Praise for Libby Fischer Hellmann

Havana Lost

"A many-layered adventure... smart writing, done in accomplished style by an author who never talks down to her readers."
—*Mystery Scene Magazine*

"A riveting historical thriller... This multigenerational page-turner is packed with intrigue and shocking plot twists."
—*Booklist*

"A sprawling tale... the story of the Cuban revolution, as well as the Cuban military efforts in Angola, is fascinating..."
—*Publishers Weekly*

"Hellmann's writing has matured considerably since her early novels. Her plotting has become more solid and assured, her characters more realistic, her settings wonderfully described. This is a fine, extremely well told novel."
—*Deadly Pleasures*

A Bitter Veil

"The Iranian revolution provides the backdrop for this meticulously researched, fast-paced stand-alone... A significant departure from the author's Chicago-based Ellie Foreman and

Georgia Davis mystery series, this political thriller will please established fans and newcomers alike."
—*Publishers Weekly*

"Hellmann crafts a tragically beautiful story... both subtle and vibrant... never sacrificing the quality of her storytelling. Instead, the message drives the psychological and emotional conflict painting a bleak and heart wrenching tale that will stick with the reader long after they finish the book."
—*Crimespree Magazine*

"Readers will be drawn in through the well-researched inside look at Iran in the late 1970s and gain perspective on what the people in that time and place endured. *A Bitter Veil* is so thought-provoking that it especially would be a great title for book clubs to discuss."
—*Book Reporter*

"*A Bitter Veil*... is a social statement about what can happen when religious fundamentalism trumps human rights, but that's hardly a drawback in this suspenseful, well-researched book. It might even serve as a warning."
—*Mystery Scene Magazine*

Set the Night on Fire

"A top-rate standalone thriller that taps into the antiwar protests of the 1960s and 70s... A jazzy fusion of past and present, Hellman's insightful, politically charged whodunit explores a fascinating period in American history."
—*Publishers Weekly*

"Superior standalone novel... Hellmann creates a fully-realized world...complete with everyday details, passions and enthusiasms on how they yearned for connection, debated about ideology and came to belief in taking risks to stand up for what they believed."
—*Chicago Tribune*

"Haunting...Rarely have history, mystery, and political philosophy blended so beautifully... could easily end up on the required reading list in college-level American History classes."
—*Mystery Scene Magazine*

Also by Libby Fischer Hellmann

Havana Lost
A Bitter Veil
Set the Night on Fire

◆

THE GEORGIA DAVIS SERIES

Nobody's Child
ToxiCity
Doubleback
Easy Innocence

◆

THE ELLIE FOREMAN SERIES

Jump Cut
A Shot to Die For
An Image of Death
A Picture of Guilt
An Eye for Murder

◆

Nice Girl Does Noir (short stories)
Chicago Blues (editor)

WAR, SPIES, AND BOBBY SOX

WAR, SPIES,
AND BOBBY SOX

STORIES ABOUT WORLD WAR II AT HOME

LIBBY FISCHER HELLMANN

THE RED HERRINGS PRESS
Chicago

"The Incidental Spy" was originally published in in 2015.
"The Day Miriam Hirsch Disappeared" was originally published in 2006.

Cover design by Miguel Ortuno
Interior design by Sue Trowbridge

Library of Congress Control Number: 2016962288

Publisher's Cataloging-In-Publication Data
(Prepared by The Donohue Group, Inc.)

Names: Hellmann, Libby Fischer.

Title: War, spies, and bobby sox : stories about World War II at home / Libby Fischer Hellmann.

Description: [Northbrook, Illinois] : [Red Herrings Press], [2017] | Contents: The incidental spy — POW — The day Miriam Hirsch disappeared.

Identifiers: ISBN 978-1-938733-97-0 | ISBN 978-1-938733-98-7 (ebook)

Subjects: LCSH: World War, 1939-1945–United States–Fiction. | World War, 1939-1945–Prisoners and prisons, German–Fiction. | Man-woman relationships–United States–Fiction. | Women spies–United States–Fiction. | Manhattan Project (U.S.)–Fiction. | Missing persons–Illinois–Chicago–Fiction. | Actresses–Illinois–Chicago–Fiction. | LCGFT: War fiction.

Classification: LCC PS3608.E46 W37 2017 | DDC 813/.6–dc23

For Mary Ellen Kazimer who knows the WWII era better than anyone ... including some who lived through it.

Table of Contents

Introduction

The volume of literature about World War II has both fascinated and intimidated me. I suspect the war's popularity as subject matter comes from the fact that it was the last time there was clarity between good and evil. The quantity and breadth of material are overwhelming—I continually wondered what I could possibly add. Still, the era has tugged at me. The first short story I wrote is set during the prewar years. In it I explored what happens to ordinary Americans in wartime. Do they become heroes or cowards? I experimented again in several other short stories. Finally, a friend suggested I try something more complex. With her encouragement, I took the plunge. The results follow: two novellas both set during the war at home. I have stitched them together with that first story, under the name *War, Spies, and Bobby Sox*. I hope you enjoy them.

The Incidental
Spy

CHAPTER 1

————————

Chicago, December, 1942

Lena was sure they were going to kill her when she climbed into the car. There were two of them this afternoon; usually it was only Hans. The second man sat in the back. He wasn't holding a knife or gun or even piano wire, but there was something chilling about him. He was a beefy, muscled bull of a man, and his presence made her colder than the December day. He refused to smile, and he wouldn't acknowledge her, as if there was a limited allocation of words and gestures, and any extra would tip the scales into chaos. And Hans, who usually liked to chat, stared straight ahead, pretending to ignore her. She felt like a ghost who'd somehow slipped into the passenger seat.

Her thoughts turned to escape. She could pull the car door handle and throw herself out onto the road. She checked the speedometer. They were cruising south on Lake Shore Drive at about thirty miles per hour. She would surely perish if she did.

————————

She might be able to slide over to Hans and stomp her foot on the brake before he could stop her. But the road was icy, and the car would skid. What if it plowed into another car? She squeezed her eyes shut. She thought about smashing the window and screaming for help, but the glass of the Ford was thick, and even if she could shatter it, what would she say? Who would believe her?

She bit her lip and tried to think. Maybe she was imagining it. Maybe it was just the stress of the past six months. Or perhaps it was her time of the month. Hadn't Karl always teased her about that? Karl. She blinked rapidly, trying to hold back the tears that still threatened at the thought of him.

It had been a routine day of typing and filing, much like all the others. She'd had lunch with Sonia, who'd poured her heart out about her husband, who'd been drafted and had fought in the Battle of Midway last summer. Walking back from the cafeteria, Lena spotted the signal, a small American flag stuck in the snow-covered urn beside the Fifty-Seventh Street florist's shop. That meant she was to meet Hans as soon as possible.

She considered ignoring it. Just not showing up. But Max was at home with Mrs. McNulty, their upstairs neighbor and babysitter. She would give him supper and make sure he went to sleep if Lena had to "work late," as she explained whenever there was a meet. She couldn't risk not meeting him. What if they retaliated against Max?

She leaned back against the seat of the Ford and swallowed. She should have run the moment she spotted the flag, scooped up Max, and boarded the first train out of Chicago. Now it was too late. She was a fool.

The Ford slowed and turned into one of the beaches off South Lake Shore Drive. Then it slowed even more. The man in the seat behind her leaned forward. She knew what was coming. She braced herself and whispered the Sh'ma.

CHAPTER 2

Berlin, May, 1935

Lena headed south on Ebertstrasse toward the Tiergarten and ducked into the park. It was the middle of May, but the hot sun made it feel more like July. Once inside the greenery, though, the temperature cooled. A breeze swished through the trees, and birds chirped, a bit frantically, Lena thought, as though they were as disturbed as she. She rounded the corner, narrowly missing a couple of girls on bicycles, braids swinging in their wake, and caught sight of several children splashing water at one another behind the rhododendrons. Josef should be waiting for her at the statue of the famous woman with her hand on her breast. Lena could never remember the woman's name.

There he was! With his wavy blond hair, sharp edge to his chin, and gorgeous green eyes, he looked Aryan, not Jewish. She, on the other hand, with her thick chestnut hair, brown eyes, and nose she thought was too big, but which Josef said he loved anyway, couldn't even try to pass. Josef claimed his looks had saved him from more than a few schoolyard brawls. His family had moved from Alsace years earlier, so he'd been French, German, and everything in between, he joked. But always in love with her, he would quickly add.

When he spotted her, he smiled broadly and opened his arms. She ran into them. He was the one for her; she'd known since they were five and she lent him a few coins at synagogue every week for *tzedukah*. But he hadn't realized it until a year ago, when they both turned sixteen. Now they were inseparable.

Lena pulled back and studied his face. She knew she wasn't smiling, and his smile, so bright a moment ago, faded. She felt her face crumple; she couldn't keep it in anymore. Tears brimmed and trickled down her cheeks.

Josef clasped her to him. "My Lena, what is wrong? Stop. All is good. We are together."

That made her cry harder.

His expression turned grim. "What? What is it?"

"Oh, Josef . . ." A strangled sob escaped.

He led her to a wrought-iron bench and made her sit. He sat beside her and grabbed her hand. Usually, the aroma of damp earth and blooming lilacs in the park made her smile, but the tears continued to stream. She tried to wipe them away with the back of her hand.

Josef brushed his fingers across her cheek. "What is wrong? You look like you've lost your best friend."

"I have," she cried.

"What are you talking about?"

She took a breath and tried to compose herself. "My parents are sending me to America. In three weeks."

Disbelief flickered across his face. "But—but your parents will be going to Budapest. With mine."

Lena felt her lips quiver. "*They* are. But they claim Hungary is not safe enough for me. They want me far away."

Josef fell silent.

"I tried to convince them to change their minds, but we have a second cousin, sort of an aunt, in Chicago who has agreed to sponsor me. It has been arranged."

"No." Josef squeezed her hand. It was just one word, but it said everything.

"I—I don't know what to do, Josef. I can't leave you."

He nodded. "Oh, *Liebchen*, I feel the same way."

She brightened for a moment. "Perhaps you could come with me."

He turned to her. "How? You know it's not possible. I would need a sponsor, and it's not so easy for us to—"

"I can ask my aunt."

"My parents would never permit it."

She cast her eyes down and whispered, "I know. But we can't stay here. We can no longer go to school. My father lost his job at the newspaper. Your father lost his government post. It will only get worse."

Josef didn't say anything for a moment. "Let me think. I will come up with something." He pulled her close and tipped up her chin with his hand. "I love you, Lena Bentheim. I always will."

"And I love you, Josef Meyer. Forever."

"Until death do us part." He leaned in and kissed her.

CHAPTER 3

Chicago, 1935

But Josef didn't come up with a plan, and three weeks later, Lena boarded a ship for New York. It was a rough voyage, and she spent most of it belowdecks, green and seasick. She vowed never to travel by sea again. Once in New York she passed through immigration, then followed the instructions in her aunt's letter and took a train bound for Chicago.

Her "aunt" Ursula met her at the station. A thin, wiry brunette with pale blue eyes, Ursula had married Erich Steiner, a math professor originally from Regensburg. They'd come to the Midwest five years earlier, when Erich was offered a position at the University of Chicago. Now, as they drove by taxi to a spacious, leafy neighborhood called Hyde Park, Lena found Ursula brisk and all business, but not unkind. Clearly, she had been making plans.

". . . English lessons . . . ," she was saying. "Typing, too, so you can get a job. We will lend you the money, of course, and you can pay us back bit by bit when you are employed. And Erich has connections at the university, so we might be able to place you there after you're qualified. The weakness in the economy still lingers, so you will be lucky to get any job at all."

Lena thanked her and gazed out the window. True, she was seventeen, an age at which many German girls left school to work or marry, but she had somehow expected—no, hoped—she would have a year or so left to study for her baccalaureate. It wasn't that she didn't want to join the adult world. It was just too soon. Three weeks earlier she and Josef were in the Tiergarten stealing kisses. Now her childhood was over. She blinked back tears.

• • •

The next six months were filled with English tutors, secretarial school, and letters from home. Josef wrote regularly, telling her about his days—he was studying at home, learning how to cook, taking long walks. He missed her terribly, he declared, and would never stop loving her. Her parents wrote cheerful letters too, never mentioning how they were coping with Hitler's restrictions. Lena knew her mother was trying to make life sound normal so Lena wouldn't worry. But the more cheerful the letter, the worse Lena knew things were. She read the newspapers. She wrote back, begging them to leave Berlin for Budapest, Paris, or New York right away. But leaving Germany was never mentioned, at least in the letters that came back.

Starting around the High Holidays, letters from Germany became less frequent. Then, in December, a letter came from Josef.

You are lucky you got out when you did. Things here are very bad. My parents left for Budapest. I don't know how much you know in America, but in September Hitler passed the Nuremberg Race Laws. These laws strip all German Jews of their citizenship. We are now "subjects" in Hitler's Reich. The laws also forbid Jews to marry or have relations with Aryans or to hire Aryan women as household help. They also presume to define how much Jewish blood makes one fully Jewish.

So, now everyone is arguing whether someone is a full Jew or part Jew. What does it matter? My father says if we stay we will be killed—they are considering even harsher laws. We will be nothing more than criminals. It is hard to believe.

Friends of my parents in Budapest have arranged for an apartment for us, but apparently it is quite small. We will leave in a few days. I miss you desperately. I have not seen your parents. Perhaps they have already left?

The next day a letter came from her mother. Unlike Josef's, it was strangely devoid of news. Just the same trivia her mother always wrote. Lena immediately replied asking why her parents hadn't left for Budapest. Had they talked to Josef? Again she begged them to leave Berlin. And then she cried.

She never got a response.

CHAPTER 4

Chicago, May, 1936

It was exactly a year later when Ursula declared Lena fit to be hired. "I was a secretary myself before we came to America, you know. That's how I met Erich. So I know all the tricks a lazy girl does to pass herself off as competent."

Lena didn't know whether that comment was directed at her, but when her aunt smiled, relief washed over her. She had learned English easily; within four months she was practically speaking like a native.

"Erich has already talked to people at the university. The Physics Department is looking for a secretary. And"—Ursula's smile broadened—"there are two German students in the department whose English is not so good. They are thrilled at having a secretary who is bilingual. Especially in today's world," she added.

Lena swallowed. "But I know nothing about physics, Aunt

Ursula. In *Gymnasium* I got most of the fundamental concepts wrong. Acceleration, rate, gravity . . . I'm hopeless."

Ursula waved a dismissive hand. "You don't need to know physics. I could barely add two and two and look where I ended up."

But Lena didn't want to meet and marry a German academician, like her aunt. Josef was waiting for her in Budapest, and as soon as she could, she would bring him to the States. In the meantime, though, she took the position.

• • •

Ryerson Physical Laboratory, a pleasant, ivy-covered building on Fifty-Eighth Street, edged one side of the university quad. Lena liked to walk through it on her way to work, imagining she was a student at the university. She wondered if she would ever reclaim those carefree days.

Although the department was small, it prided itself on two Nobel Prizes won by its scientists, one of whom, Arthur Compton, was the department chair. She quickly learned that Ursula was right about one thing. She didn't need to know anything about physics.

The one imperative was to make sure her typing was accurate. Most of the documents contained columns of symbols and fractions and percentages that, while a mystery to her, were known to the scientists, so it was critical to get them right. When she asked why, Professor Compton explained that the department's mission was to instill the habit of careful, intelligent observation of the external world.

"In order to do that," he said, fingering the small mustache that looked a little too much like Hitler's, Lena thought, "we expect our graduate students to replicate classical experiments by eminent investigators. And that includes the data they observe and analyze."

Lena nodded. She was intimidated by Compton but more relaxed around the students. They chatted and laughed and traded jokes that were surprisingly funny for scientists. There were the two German graduate students who had come to America a year earlier and soon depended on her to help write their papers. A young Brit and three Americans also hung around.

"There are actually three of us Germans," Franz told her one day. "But Karl is at Columbia University in New York for the semester."

"Why?" Lena asked.

The second German, Heinrich, smiled. "That's where the action is. They're doing lots of exciting atomic experiments. I can't wait for him to come back and tell us everything."

Thankfully, Lena knew what an atom was. "But why are they experimenting with the atom?"

"Splitting it," Franz said. "Even Einstein thinks it might be possible."

"To what end?"

"The experts claim if they succeed, a great deal of energy will be released."

"Energy?"

"Heat. Light. Radiation. An explosion more fiery than man has ever known."

"A bomb?"

"Perhaps. But they say Hitler is doing the same thing. So, of course, the Americans must hurry . . ." His voice trailed off. "At any rate, Karl will be back in September."

CHAPTER 5

Chicago, September, 1936

By fall Josef's letters were less frequent. He was fine, he said in the one letter she received. His mother was sick. When she coughed, her handkerchief was tinged with blood, and they feared it was tuberculosis. But he was working with a carpenter in Budapest and learning a trade. "Think how useful that will be when we build our house."

She wanted to share his optimism, but she hadn't heard from her parents in months, and Josef said he hadn't seen them in Budapest. The émigré German Jewish community there was small; everyone knew one another. She had heard the rumors about the SS rounding up Jews and sending them to forced labor camps. She prayed that wasn't the case and that she would soon receive a joyful letter from Paris or London or Amsterdam.

One afternoon she was in the filing room, a cramped closet, when a male voice called out from the front.

"Halloo. Is anyone there?" It was a tentative voice, speaking heavily accented English that sounded like that of a German national. Bavarian, actually. Lena had learned how to figure out what part of Germany someone was from by the way they spoke English.

She hurried out. A young man with dark curly hair and glasses that magnified his brown eyes leaned against a wall. He was about six feet—she was using feet and inches in her calculations now—and solidly built.

"How can I help you?" she said, knowing her own accent marked her as a foreigner.

His face lit. "You are German!" Something about his expression, so innocent and yet full of delight, instantly put her at ease.

She nodded. "And you are from Bavaria."

He switched to German. "How did you know?"

She tapped her lips. "I hear it."

He smiled back. "You have a good ear." He raised his palm. "Munich."

"Berlin." She did the same.

"Do you work here?"

"I am the department secretary. Since last May." She tilted her head. "Are you new?"

He laughed. "No. But I have been away."

"Oh. You are Karl."

He brightened even more. "Yes."

"You have been at Columbia in New York."

He nodded. "And you?"

She held up her hand. "As I said, I am not a student."

"Your name." There was a softness in his voice as he said it.

She felt a flush creep across her face. "Of course. Lena Bentheim."

He offered his hand. "Karl Stern."

She took it. Stern could be a Jewish name. They stood with their hands clasped a beat too long. Neither appeared to mind.

• • •

Karl came to the physics office for a different reason every day. He needed a book from the library—she often checked them out for the students. He needed to find a paper someone else had written. He lost his schedule of classes for the fall. Lena looked forward to his visits.

Two weeks later he mustered up the courage to ask her to tea.

"Tea? How—lovely." She giggled. "But we are not in London."

"Yes, of course." He flushed from the neck up. "Coffee, then."

She cocked her head. "Not in Vienna either, although it is true that Americans are in love with their coffee."

Karl's face turned crimson. He stammered. "Well—well, then, I apologize for—for . . ." His voice faded and he seemed to shrink into himself.

"But beer." Lena smiled. "Now, that's another matter. Do you think we might find a nearby tavern?"

Karl's face glowed.

"Come back at five, yah?" she said.

He nodded enthusiastically.

Lena took him to a restaurant just off campus. The menu boasted the Budweiser logo and the words "Makes Good Food Taste Better" at the top. The tavern offered thick soups, meat loaf, and even hamburgers at prices students could afford. All washed down with beer. The pleasant smell of grease drifted through the air; Lena's mouth watered. They both ordered the meat loaf.

They talked about everything but focused on what was happening in Germany. The Berlin Olympic Games had just ended, and Hitler had taken a keen interest, hoping his Aryan athletes would dominate the competitions. It was the irony of ironies that Jesse Owens, a Negro from America, won all four of his events. Because of the games, moreover, the German government had temporarily refrained from actions against Jews.

"But more restrictions are on the way," Karl said.

Lena sat back. "Are you Jewish?"

"Of course. I thought you knew."

She leaned against the back of her chair. A deep wave of relief passed through her. Karl understood. The other German graduate students were sympathetic, but they weren't Jewish. It wasn't the same. For the first time since she'd come to America she realized how guarded she'd been.

"Where are your parents?" she asked. "And the rest of your family?"

"In Austria. I am trying to get them here. I think it will happen, but I don't know when. The US has become quite restrictive about who can get in." He paused. "What about yours?"

She hesitated, then shook her head. "I don't know."

He reached across the table and squeezed her hand.

CHAPTER 6

By the end of the year Lena and Karl were a couple. She spent more time at his apartment, a shabby room in the southern part of Hyde Park, than at Ursula and Erich's, but Ursula didn't seem to mind. It was as if her aunt knew what was happening and tacitly approved. Karl was invited to Shabbos dinner every Friday; it became the only big meal they ate, except when they went out.

The night she and Karl made love for the first time, she had the feeling she was his first. Afterward she knew she had to write Josef. At first she had been wracked with guilt and had tried to keep Karl at a distance. But he was so unassuming, gentle, and smart, she soon developed feelings for him. There had been no letter from Josef in months. Memories of him were fading like dried flowers inside a book, a book that had been written centuries earlier.

Meanwhile the Physics Department was suffused with an enthusiasm that hadn't been present before. Compton, the head of the department, was known for studying cosmic rays, but the experiments that intrigued the students were those Enrico Fermi started in 1934 in Europe.

One night, after they made love, Karl tried to explain Fermi's work in a way Lena could understand. "It has to do with bombarding elements with neutrons. One of the elements Fermi uses is uranium, which is one of the heaviest of the known elements."

"Why is that important?" Lena asked.

"Because the result turned out to be lighter than the elements he'd started with."

She frowned. "What do you mean?"

"Fermi himself didn't really understand why, but others were quick to link it to Einstein's theory of $E = mc2$."

"Why?"

Karl grinned. "Because a great deal of energy was released during the bombardment." He paused. "When we figure out exactly how it happened and what exactly was released, a new world of possibilities will emerge."

Lena loved to listen to Karl. She barely understood what he was talking about, but his eagerness and love of learning kindled a desire in her to go back to school. To finish what they called, in the States, high school. Maybe, afterward, she would even enroll at the university.

CHAPTER 7

Chicago, 1937-1938

The day Lena and Karl married was a warm, breezy day in June 1937. The tiny wedding at KAM Isaiah Israel synagogue in Hyde Park included fewer than a dozen guests: Ursula and Erich, the graduate students in the Physics Department, a secretary, Bonnie, from the Math Department with whom Lena was friends, and Professor Compton and his wife. Lena had bought a white dress on sale at Marshall Field's, and Bonnie had helped her make a veil. But what she loved most were her white sandals with rhinestone bows, which sparkled in the light, making her feel as though she were floating above the ground.

After the ceremony, Ursula and Erich invited everyone to their house for wedding cake and champagne. Ursula surprised Lena with a marzipan cake from Lutz's, the German bakery; her aunt had gone all the way to the North Side to pick it up. Later that evening, Karl's friends took them to a special performance of the

Benny Goodman Trio at the Congress Hotel, and they kicked up their heels until the wee hours. Lena couldn't have asked for a more perfect day. If only her parents had been there to see it.

• • •

A few months later, as they walked to the quad from their apartment near Fifty-Seventh and Dorchester, Lena—now Mrs. Stern—held up her hand, watching her wedding ring flash this way and that in the morning sun. She did that a lot now. To most people, it was just a modest gold band, but to her it was as valuable as the whole of the recently built Fort Knox.

She turned to her husband. "Thank you, Karl."

"For what?"

"For everything. You made me whole again. I finally belong."

He smiled and reached for her hand. They walked a few steps in silence. Then, "I have a confession to make," she said.

"What, my darling?"

"I wish . . ." She hesitated. "Sometimes I just want to forget what's going on in Europe. I just want to think about our life here. Does that make me a terrible person?"

He squeezed her hand. "I do not think so. I do it as well sometimes."

"Doesn't it make you feel guilty?"

"I don't let it. And I take heart that I am working in a field that could end the suffering there."

"But that's so far in the future . . . and so unsure, given how powerful the Nazis have become."

He took her arm. "Perhaps. Perhaps not. And don't forget, Lena, my darling, you are helping, too."

"I'm not doing anything except typing and filing and writing letters."

He touched her lips with his index finger. "Don't say that. Your work allows us to concentrate on our research. And that research might well give America a valuable tool one day." He leaned over and kissed her. Lena wanted to collect moments like this, if only to store them in life's album of happy times.

So Lena tried to ignore the steady drip of bad news from Europe. It worked for a while, but like a leaky faucet, the bad news was unrelenting. Hungary was pressured to join the Axis; reportedly, Jews outside Budapest were being rounded up. Lena prayed that Josef stayed safe. She wouldn't let herself think about her parents. She tried to persuade herself that whether they were at a labor camp or had been sent to what were now called concentration camps, *she* was in America, and America was interested in America, not Europe. Sometimes it even worked.

America was focused on rebuilding its economy and staying out of the war. Of course, people like Henry Ford disparaged Jews, as did Father Coughlin, a Catholic priest whose weekly radio program drew millions of listeners. She would turn off the radio when his show began.

• • •

In March 1938, the Nazis overran Austria and annexed it to Germany. By October they had invaded the Sudetenland, and November brought Kristallnacht. It was no longer possible to ignore what was happening. Europe was an ugly carcass filled with violence and death.

But the physics community of which she was now a part celebrated good news. Enrico Fermi was awarded the 1938 Nobel

Prize for his work in neutron bombardment, and that made everyone optimistic about the future of nuclear research.

By December Lena had missed a period, and her breasts had grown tender. She knew from repeated discussions with Bonnie that she was pregnant. She wasn't sure how Karl would take it—he had been working such long hours—so she surprised him one evening and took him to the restaurant with the Budweiser menu. It had become their "spot."

"I have news," she said after they'd ordered beers.

Karl cocked his head. "About your parents?"

She shook her head. "No. Nothing like that."

His brow furrowed. "Then, what?"

She reached for his hand. "We're going to have a baby."

Karl blinked as if he hadn't understood.

"You. And me. We're going to have a child."

A glorious smile unfolded across his face.

• • •

Just before Christmas, two scientists announced they had replicated Fermi's experiments. They had bombarded uranium atoms that threw off neutrons and energy. Under the right circumstances, they claimed, these "boiled-off" neutrons might collide with other atoms in a chain reaction and release even more neutrons and energy. They called it "fission."

The scientists were from Berlin.

CHAPTER 8

Chicago, 1939

In March of 1939 Hitler seized Czechoslovakia. Neville Chamberlain spoke of appeasement, and so many people wanted to believe him that the voices begging the world to stop Hitler went unheard.

A month later Karl came home, a wide grin on his face. Lena was simmering bean soup. Thick, the way he liked it.

"You look like that cat in *Alice in Wonderland*."

"You'll never believe it!" he said.

"What? What is it?"

"I've just had a letter from my parents."

Her eyes widened. Letters from loved ones in Nazi-occupied countries were rare. "And?"

"Next month they will board a ship in Hamburg and sail to Cuba!"

Her mouth fell open. "Really?"

He nodded eagerly. "The ship will carry almost one thousand Jewish refugees. They will stay in Havana for a while, and after that—"

She cut him off. "We can bring them here!" She waved the wooden spoon she'd been using to stir the soup. "How wonderful!"

"They say to expect a telegram from Havana toward the end of May."

"Karl. We must celebrate."

"Yes." His soft brown eyes were shining. "I think rum. Do we have any?"

She giggled. "No, but I will go out and get some. This is wonderful news."

"They will love you."

She gave him a shy smile. He hugged her, then patted her stomach, which, at six months, was nicely rounded. "And when the baby comes—"

Lena cut in again. "What's the name of this magic ship?"

"The *St. Louis.*"

• • •

The ship sailed from Hamburg on May 13. Lena and Karl made preparations. They decided his parents would take their bedroom until they found their own place. Karl and Lena would sleep in the living room. They bought a used couch that opened into a bed. Lena planned menus for two weeks and brought home grocery bags stuffed with food.

The ship was due to land in Havana on May 27. But the day passed with no telegram from Karl's parents. When there was still no word by evening the next day, they began to worry.

The story didn't take long to emerge. Once the ship entered Cuban waters, Cuba's pro-Fascist president, Federico Laredo Brú, decided to ignore the refugees' documents. Only twenty-two of one thousand Jews were allowed to enter Cuba. The rest were forced to stay on the ship. The refugees appealed to America to let them in, and a chorus of voices on both sides of the issue joined in. There were marches, hundreds of letters written to FDR, poignant stories about the refugees on the ship.

There were also those who demanded the ship and its cargo be turned away. Negotiations between Cuba, the US, and even the Dominican Republic seesawed with good news one day, bad news the next. It seemed as if the entire world was holding its breath.

Ultimately, the naysayers prevailed. On June 7, negotiations failed, and the *St. Louis* was forced to return to Europe. Lena and Karl were devastated. Karl sank into such a severe depression that Lena worried he might do something crazy. She hid the kitchen knives in the back of the cabinet.

Several European countries eventually took in some of the refugees, but those who went to Belgium, France, or the Netherlands were trapped when Hitler invaded those countries a year later. A few months after the ship returned to Europe, Karl got a letter from his parents. They had settled in France. That was the last time he heard from them.

● ● ●

At the beginning of August, Albert Einstein wrote a letter to FDR. In it, he summarized the latest scientific thinking on chain reactions, uranium, and fission. Then he wrote:

This new phenomenon would also lead to the construction of bombs, and it is conceivable—though much less certain—that extremely powerful bombs of this type may thus be constructed.

On September 1, Hitler invaded Poland. Two days later England and France declared war against Germany.

CHAPTER 9

_____

Chicago, 1939-41

Max Stern was born two days later, on September 5, 1939. Lena had an easy labor: her water broke at noon; by seven, Max made his appearance. He was a perfect baby boy: dark hair and lots of it, a lusty cry, and a determined chin that said he would not be ignored. They named him after Lena's father, Maximilian—who, if not already dead, was clearly lost to Lena.

Lena took her time recovering, so Karl organized the *bris*. He found the *mohel*, invited the guests, ordered trays of food. Lena spent the entire time in the bedroom with Ursula. The baby gave a sharp cry when the *mohel*'s scalpel sliced his foreskin. Lena ran to the bathroom and threw up.

Max was the most adored baby ever. Lena thought of him as a little prince and, of course, quit her job to take care of him. She was determined to become the mother he deserved. After all, his birth was proof that the Nazis, no matter what, had not prevailed. It was her job to make sure it stayed that way.

Over the next year she carefully washed his diapers and bottles, made sure he had plenty of fresh air, and sang and talked to him constantly. The experts said the more you talked to your baby, the smarter he would be.

Still, in the dark hours of the night, she was beset with fear. A mere sniffle meant a rush to the doctor. She worried whether she was feeding him enough. Whether he was sleeping too much or too little. Even a diaper rash made her nervous. In the deepest, darkest part of her brain, she was sure that one mistake, one careless error on her part, would mean the end. Karl, who had bounced back from his depression over the *St. Louis*, tried to comfort her, but her outlook, so broad before, shrank into a tiny worldview of what Max needed, what Max did, how Max fared. His powdery baby smell was the most seductive aroma she could imagine.

Max was asleep one summer night in July 1940 when Karl got home. Lena usually tried to keep Max up to see his father, but tonight his little head drooped, his eyes closed, and she had to put him to bed. It didn't help that Karl was often late now that research on chain reactions and uranium compounds had picked up.

Much of the new work, he told her, was done in Berkeley, New York, and Britain, but Compton was the head of the National Academy of Sciences, and his opinion was sought on everything dealing with nuclear research. That meant lots of staff papers, analyses, and theoretical discussions that lasted until the middle of the night.

Lena had climbed into bed herself and was nodding off when

Karl came into the bedroom. She could smell his beery breath across the room. Karl rarely drank. She decided to ignore him, but when he stumbled over his shoes and let out a yelp, she switched on a lamp and rose onto her elbows.

"Are you all right, darling?"

"Yah, yah," he replied.

"You're drunk."

"Quite possibly." He let out a loud burp as if to prove the point.

Lena shook her head in mock annoyance. She couldn't be angry with Karl.

"It was a crazy day. Some of us went out for a few beers to calm down."

Lena pushed herself to a sitting position. If Karl needed a few beers to calm down, this was important. "Why don't I make you some coffee?"

"Thank you, *Liebchen.*"

Ten minutes later, she brought a steaming cup into the bedroom, handed it to her husband, and got back into bed. She watched as he took a few cautious sips. A few minutes passed. Karl's furrowed brow smoothed out, and he looked calmer.

"So," she said. "What happened?"

He sat on the edge of the bed. "I will tell you. But first, you must take an oath that you will never repeat any of this to anyone."

"Of course," she said. "Remember, I used to work there."

He nodded. "I remember. Did you ever meet an army officer, Colonel Charles Collins? He came to the department often once the government created the Uranium Committee." Karl fingered the sheet Lena had draped around herself, as if he could feel Lena's skin through it. "He always demanded to meet with

Compton privately. As if he was in charge and Compton worked for him."

"I don't recall him. Was he a scientist?"

"Not really. He took a course or two in college, Compton said, but he thought he knew it all."

"Just like an officer. They put on a uniform and think they rule the world," Lena said. "They are the same the world over. Why did Compton put up with him?"

"I wondered the same thing. It turns out he didn't." Karl smiled.

"How do you mean?"

"So." Karl grabbed his coffee and took another sip. "I don't know if I told you, but in May—well, this gets rather complicated—the Germans seized one of the largest heavy-water production plants. It's in Norway."

"Heavy water?"

"It's a type of water that can help build nuclear weapons. It showed the world that Germany is serious about producing an atomic weapon."

Lena nodded.

"Things at work accelerated quickly after that. The Brits and the Americans do not want to fall behind, you see."

A flash of irritation washed over her. "Yes, but what does this have to do with you getting drunk?"

"I'm getting to that." He dropped his knee and ran his hand down the sheet that covered her, stopped at her breast, and cupped it. She was still nursing Max, and her breasts were heavy and full.

She flicked his hand away. "Well?"

He sighed. "Well, last month the government reorganized its nuclear research program. They're looking into several different ways to separate isotopes and produce a chain reaction. But the key is that military representatives will no longer be on the committee." He paused. "So when Collins came in today, he was told he had no further reason to come into the department." Karl grinned.

"And?"

"The colonel was not happy."

"I don't understand. What does it mean, no more military on the committee?"

"In practice, it does not mean much. It's just so that we can get enough funds to focus on the science without depending on the military for budget approval. But clearly, they will not be excluded for long. Whatever we come up with, they're going to implement."

"But Collins wasn't satisfied?"

"What do the Americans say?" He switched to English. "Not for a 'New York minute'?" He went back to German. "He became belligerent, started to make threats, said he would go to the top to complain. That the military *should* be in charge of us."

"With him as leader, no doubt," Lena said.

Karl nodded. "Of course. Then he stomped out."

Lena mulled it over. "My goodness. Such excitement!"

"At any rate, Compton stayed in his office for a while. Then he came out and gave us a stern lecture on confidentiality. He said it was vital that no one know anything about our work. Including our families. That everything we do is a matter of the utmost national security. To be held in the strictest secrecy." Karl bit his lip. "If he finds out I told you this much, he will fire me."

"I will tell no one. You know that."

"Yah, I know." He caressed her cheek. "So, that's why we went drinking. We were all a bit—how do they say in English?—shaky. Suddenly, we are not at all sure what the future holds."

Lena slipped her arms around her husband. "Don't worry. I will not pry any secrets out of you. Now, come to bed."

CHAPTER 10

Chicago, 1941

By the time Max was eighteen months, Lena did something she should have done years earlier. One night in March 1941, she wrote to Josef. She had no idea if he was still at the Budapest address she had for him, but she told him about Karl, Max, her life in America, and the Physics Department. She apologized for not writing sooner. She didn't know how to explain. Their love had made sense during the traumatic years in Berlin. He had been her lighthouse, the beacon of her hope. But she had moved on. She didn't say that in the letter; she simply said she hoped he could forgive her. She didn't expect him to respond, but she felt better for writing.

To her surprise, a month later she received a reply. Josef was still in Budapest. His mother had passed and his father was frail, but he wanted her to know he understood. "Time releases no one," he said. "Life always changes."

In fact, he was seeing a woman himself, and the letter Lena had written he took as a reprieve. He intended to ask this woman to marry him. He wished Lena nothing but the best for her and her family. Lena's eyes filled as she read the letter. At the same time, her guilt lifted. She felt lighter than she had in years.

As spring advanced into summer, Max was starting to talk, and his conversations, peppered with real words as well as baby talk, were a delight. Lena chatted with him most of the day, and both Lena and Karl were convinced he was an intellectual giant.

One afternoon, on a beautiful summer day that reminded her of the day they were married—it was hard to believe it had been four years already—she wheeled Max in a newfangled baby stroller to a park adjacent to South Lake Shore Drive. Now that the north and south legs of the drive were connected, it was busier than ever, and they crossed the street carefully. Lena meandered down to the beach at Fifty-Ninth Street and spread a blanket over the sand. She and Max spent the afternoon building sand castles and dipping their toes in the frigid water.

When it was time for Max's nap, she put him down on the blanket and lay down beside him. She must have dozed off too, because the next thing Lena remembered, the sun was peeking through the trees from the west. She checked her watch; they had been asleep for two hours.

Hurriedly, she roused Max. He wanted to go back to the water. She clutched his hand and made one more trip to the edge of the lake, then settled him in the stroller for the journey back home.

As she made her way from the beach back to Fifty-Seventh Street, Lena had the sense she was being followed. She whipped around but didn't see anyone. She frowned. Max chattered away; she had to focus on him. She kept going. Once they'd crossed

Fifty-Seventh Street to the sidewalk, the feeling intensified. She spun around again. This time she caught the shadow of a figure melting into the narrow space between two buildings. Someone *was* following them.

But who? Hyde Park was one of the safest neighborhoods in Chicago. She began rolling Max's stroller so quickly that Max started to fret. She tried to shush him, explaining they had slept so long they were late getting dinner. Max seemed to understand, because he stopped crying.

The feeling faded as she passed the shops of Hyde Park, but she was still wary. She kept looking around; no one seemed interested in her. She forced herself to stop in at the butcher's for a veal roast. Then she bought small potatoes and fresh green beans at the market two doors down. At the last moment, she added ripe tomatoes.

Back home she locked the door, something she rarely did, and turned on the radio. It was filled with war news, none of it good. She started preparing dinner, wondering who had been following her and why. She was certain it was a man; she'd seen a flash of dark pants and a striped shirt.

When Karl got home, she told him.

Karl frowned. "You have no idea who it was?"

She shook her head.

He looked like he was seriously thinking. Then he looked up. "Are you sure?"

She shot him an irritated glance. "Of course. Do you think I would make this up?"

"No. But I cannot believe it was intentional. Perhaps it was a hobo who wanted your money."

She shook her head. "He did not make a move toward my wallet."

"In that case, I have no idea, *Liebchen*. Maybe forget it. It might have been"—Karl shrugged—"a prank? A mistake?"

"And if it happens again?"

"We will deal with it," he said firmly.

She kept her mouth shut.

CHAPTER 11

December 7, a chilly Chicago Sunday, changed everything. Lena and Karl had put Max down for a nap. Lena decided to make a batch of latkes for Hanukkah, which would start in a week's time. She was looking forward to the fact that Max might actually understand some of what the holiday was about this year.

Karl was working from home. He was not supposed to bring home any materials from the office, but he never discussed them with Lena, and she didn't ask. Otherwise, Lena and Max might never have seen him—he was so absorbed in his research. In July, a report from the British indicated that a nuclear weapon was a distinct possibility, and the Brits were going ahead with development.

Their enthusiasm spurred the Americans to reanalyze their findings. In November, Compton's committee concluded that a critical mass of between two and one hundred kilograms of uranium 235 would produce a powerful fission bomb, and that for fifty to one hundred million dollars it could be built.

Lena, who was chopping onions and enjoying their aroma, turned on the radio. The Bears football game was on. The broadcast was interrupted around one thirty p.m. with the news that the Japanese were bombing the Pacific Fleet in Pearl Harbor, Hawaii. Lena clapped a hand over her mouth. Karl stopped working and they remained glued to the radio for the rest of the day. Nearly twenty American ships, including eight enormous battleships, and almost two hundred airplanes were destroyed. More than two thousand American soldiers and sailors died; another thousand were wounded.

A day later, while officials were still sorting out the damage, FDR went to Congress and delivered a short speech calling December 7 "a date which will live in infamy." Barely an hour later, Congress declared war on Japan. Three days after that the country was at war with Germany.

Lena descended into an unremitting state of anxiety. America was on the right side, but nothing was certain. She knew that events could—and did—change in an instant. The anti-Semitic laws in Europe, her flight from Germany, the loss of Josef, her parents' silence, Kristallnacht. She felt powerless, like a tennis ball buffeted back and forth across the net, with no will of its own. The security she'd been able to create with Karl and Max rested on the precarious feathers of history. The slightest change in their lives could scatter those feathers to oblivion.

Ironically, her mood was at odds with that of the rest of the country. Bravado and cheerfulness prevailed, as though Americans were relieved, excited, even cocky, about going to war. "Slap the Japs" could be heard in bars, people talked about "Jap-hunting" licenses, and reprisals against Japanese-Americans began.

Japanese restaurants closed, their shop windows smashed. Americans boycotted everything Japanese, and there was much cheering and jeering from Chinatown, Japan's sworn enemy. Lena couldn't help comparing what was happening in America to what she'd gone through in Germany, although it wasn't nearly as harsh. She was frightened at the prospect of war, but she couldn't make herself hate the Japanese people.

Still, as the country geared up, she went through her days silent and brooding, waiting for something else to happen. Something bad was coming. She couldn't sleep, couldn't eat, couldn't sit still. Even Max picked up on her tension and grew cranky.

• • •

It happened a week later. A layer of sleet glazed everything with a coating of ice. By evening it was covered by two inches of snow. The roads were covered with a deceptive white shroud. Karl would be walking home from the university, but he had no boots or scarf; the morning had been unusually sunny and mild for December. He was rarely home before midnight since Pearl Harbor anyway, so Lena didn't wait up.

She woke a few hours later and checked the time. It was one in the morning, but Karl wasn't in bed beside her. He hadn't called either, which he usually did if he was going to be very late or decided to spend the night at the office. She peered out the window. More snow. He must be staying overnight at the department, she told herself. No one would be foolish enough to go out in this storm. She went back to bed.

She was startled awake by the insistent ringing of the doorbell. She looked at the clock. Three a.m. Had Karl forgotten his key?

He never had before. She wrapped her robe tightly around her, went to the door, and squinted through the peephole. Two police officers stood outside, stamping their feet in the snow. Her pulse thundered in her ears, coursing through her hands, chest, and head. It was hard to breathe. What did they want? Were they coming for her? Or Karl? Why?

For an instant she was back in Nazi Germany. But this was America. Karl had suggested she keep a gun in the house. She'd refused, telling him they were safe here. That even the thought of a weapon was ridiculous. Now she wasn't so sure.

She cracked open the door, her hands trembling. "Yes?" Her voice was a hoarse whisper.

"Are you Mrs. Stern?"

She swallowed and nodded.

"I'm Officer O'Grady. And this is my partner, Officer Maywood. May we come in?"

"What do you want?"

"We need to talk to you about your husband."

Lena's stomach clenched, and she sagged against the door. Suddenly all she wanted to do was hurry back to bed and pull the covers over her head.

"Please, ma'am. Could you open the door?" O'Grady hesitated, as if he knew she was afraid. "We mean you no harm."

She sized up the officers. Bundled up in overcoats, boots, and gloves, they didn't appear to be carrying weapons. In fact, the one called O'Grady took off his cap. Snowflakes melted on its brim. She opened the door wider.

"Thank you, ma'am." They came in and stood just inside the doorway. She closed it and planted herself in front of it.

"I'm afraid we have some bad news, Mrs. Stern."

A steel band wrapped itself around her head.

"Your husband is Karl Stern?"

She nodded.

O'Grady took a breath. It sounded like a sigh. "We responded to a call of an accident in the snow. It was a hit-and-run. On Fifty-Seventh Street."

The steel band tightened. Lena felt rooted to the floor.

"About an hour ago your husband was walking east on Fifty-Seventh Street. We believe he was coming from the university. That—"

She cut him off. "What happened?"

O'Grady looked down, away, then met her gaze. "Your husband was hit by an automobile. The driver must have lost control on the ice. The car hit him broadside. I'm sorry, Mrs. Stern, he didn't make it. He's dead."

CHAPTER 12

———————

Chicago, 1941-1942

Hashem was punishing Lena. He must be. At some point God must have ordained that she would never be happy for long. Was it because of the kisses she and Josef stole behind the trees in the Tiergarten? Because she had survived and her parents apparently had not? Perhaps it was because she hadn't put enough faith in him over the years. She had worked to create her own life, her own happiness. It was clear now that God did not approve.

She endured the funeral, thick clouds of grief fogging her mind. The interment, too. Ursula organized the *shivah*, and for seven days people filed in and out. Compton came several times, sat with her, and held her hand. She didn't remember his words; all she recalled was that his glasses picked up the reflection of the lamp across the room. The German students from the department, scientists themselves now, came. So did her friend,

Bonnie, from the Math Department, and people she didn't know who said they knew Karl.

Max couldn't understand where Papa had gone. He must be hiding, he said, and hunted for him under the beds, in the closets, behind doors. He kept asking her when Papa would be back. At one point he asked, "Papa fight war?"

Lena's jaw dropped. Max wasn't even three years old. How was he able to make a connection between the war and his father's disappearance? She tried to explain.

"No, *Liebchen*. Papa has gone to heaven."

"When come back?"

The lump in her throat was so thick she thought it might choke her. "He's not."

She gathered Max in her arms and hugged him tight. At the same time, she couldn't help thinking how her life had been marked by momentous yet horrific events. Max was born a few days after war was declared. Now Karl had been killed a few days after Pearl Harbor. What was next?

Officers O'Grady and Maywood were replaced by a detective accompanied by a man who introduced himself as FBI Special Agent Pete Lanier. Lena stiffened. Probably in his forties, he was tall and lean and bald. But the expression in his brown eyes was curiously kind. Still.

"FBI? Why are you here?"

He smiled. "It's just a formality. We keep tabs on everyone at the lab."

"Why?" Lena asked.

"There are some very special people working there," he said amiably.

Lena didn't respond.

The detective told Lena they'd canvassed the neighborhood, but no one recalled a car sliding across Fifty-Seventh Street at two in the morning. Everyone had been tucked up in bed. But they would keep looking, the detective promised. She saw in his eyes that he was lying. She spun around to Lanier. His eyebrows arched.

• • •

The end-of-the-year holidays were desolate. Lena remembered how she and Karl would spend New Year's Eve with the other physicists in the department. They would go up to the Loop to hear jazz or swing music and dance until midnight. Not this year. Ursula brought over chicken and red cabbage, but it went untouched.

Two weeks later Ursula rang the doorbell. It was well past noon, but Lena hadn't bothered to dress herself or Max. In her usual efficient way, Ursula made them bathe and put on clothes. Then she cleaned the house and made tea.

When they were seated at the kitchen table, Ursula stirred sugar into her tea. "So, my dear, what are your plans?"

Lena looked up, trying to blink away the fog. She shrugged.

Ursula nodded. "Yes. You have been through hell. Still, it is time to think about moving forward."

Lena groped for a reply, but it seemed as if Ursula was speaking a foreign language. She had no idea what to say.

Ursula went on. "It has been over thirty days since Karl passed. I know you're still grieving, but it is time to start picking up your life."

Lena kept her mouth shut.

"What is your money situation?"

"We are scraping by."

"So," Ursula said in a matter-of-fact tone, "you will need to go back to work."

"How can I? What about Max?"

"We will find someone to look after him. Perhaps the lady who lives upstairs. The one whose grandchildren come every week?"

Mrs. McNulty, a blowsy woman with flyaway white hair, lived upstairs. She never forgot to wink at Max whenever she saw him, and she always asked Lena how he was. In fact, Lena remembered her concerned expression among the sea of faces at the *shivah*. She'd brought down a bowl of fruit, Lena recalled. Apples, Max's favorite.

"But where? How can I make enough to support us both? And pay Mrs. McNulty?"

Ursula stared at Lena for a few seconds in silence, then pursed her lips. "Surely you remember."

"Remember what?"

"Professor Compton. He sat beside you for a long while one night at the *shivah*. He said your old job was waiting for you if you wanted it."

Lena shook her head. She had no memory of the conversation.

"I was right beside you, rubbing your back. He even said he understood you could not work late because of Max. He said you and he could work something out. They replaced you with another secretary, of course, but he said he could use a second as well."

Lena's eyes widened.

"It's time," Ursula said.

CHAPTER 13

And so Lena went back to her job at the Physics Department. It had never been a quiet place, but it was positively bustling now, a frantic urgency sweeping the air. Ever since America had entered the war, each day felt like a race against the clock.

Compton was at the helm, spearheading experiments in fission from coast to coast. Each project, from Enrico Fermi's at Columbia University in New York to J. Robert Oppenheimer's at Berkeley, would, they hoped, forge a path to a nuclear device. Lena and Sonia, the other secretary, kept busy sending frequent letters, sometimes telegrams, to the scientists; typing conclusions and analyses by other physicists; even corresponding with government officials. Lena was thrilled to be interacting, albeit indirectly, with the most famous scientists in the country. Bit by bit, she started to emerge from her shell of grief.

Shortly after she returned, Compton decided to combine some of the research programs into one location. He appointed Leo Szilard head of materials acquisition and convinced Szilard,

Fermi, and others to move to Chicago. He snagged some unused space beneath a racquetball court under the west grandstand of Stagg Field and created what became known as the Metallurgical Lab. It was here that the department would build the machinery to conduct experiments with graphite and uranium, which would, they hoped, produce a chain reaction when bombarded with neutrons.

At home, life seemed to fall into place as well. Max enjoyed his days with Mrs. McNulty, whom he called Mrs. M.

"All he wants to eat are apples," Mrs. M said.

"That's not necessarily bad," Lena said.

Mrs. McNulty smiled. "And when he's not munching on the fruit, he plays with Lincoln Logs. I think he's going to be an engineer when he grows up. Or a scientist."

"Like his father," Lena said softly.

She tried to spend as much time as she could with Max after work and begged Mrs. McNulty to let him nap long hours so she could keep him up at night. He was chattering nonstop now, and Lena loved teaching him new words and ideas. But even with a three-hour nap, his little head drooped by nine in the evening, so she would sing him some of the German lullabies her mother sang to her, tuck him in bed, then fall asleep herself.

Between food, rent, and Mrs. McNulty, Lena was barely making it financially. Every week she plunged deeper in debt. The kindly grocer extended endless lines of credit; Mrs. McNulty, too. Still, Lena worried she could never repay what she owed. She feared it was just a matter of time until her life unraveled completely.

CHAPTER 14

April, 1942—Chicago

Lena picked up the phone at work one rainy morning just before lunch. Compton had been expecting a call from Fermi, who was in the midst of moving to Chicago. When he called, she was to find Compton immediately. So she was expecting a male voice on the other end of the line. Instead she heard a sobbing woman, whose obvious anguish made her words incomprehensible.

"Hello? Who is this?"

More crying, followed by a sharp intake of breath.

"Please, who is there?"

"M-Mrs. Stern," she stammered. "It's—it's Mabel McNulty."

It took Lena a moment to register the caller. They always addressed each other as Mrs. Stern or Mrs. M. But when she realized who it was, a bolt of fear streaked up her spine. "What's the matter? Is Max all right?"

"The—the police are here."

Panic surged through Lena. She began to shiver uncontrollably. "The police? What happened?"

"Mrs. Stern, I can't believe it." Her voice cracked. "I don't know—I just don't know how it happened."

"Mrs. McNulty," Lena was shouting now, so loud that Sonia looked up from her desk in alarm. "Where is Max?"

A fresh stream of crying filled her ears. Lena jumped up. With her free hand she grabbed her purse. A *swish* came over the telephone line, and a deep male voice said, "Mrs. Stern? This is Officer Delgado. Chicago Police Department."

Lena's stomach clenched, and a wave of nausea worked its way up to her throat.

"Your boy, Max—has been kidnapped. We're sending a squad car to pick you up."

• • •

Mrs. McNulty and Max were on their way back from the Museum of Science and Industry, where Max loved to wander through the *Coal Mine* exhibit, Mrs. M said. She had brought the stroller in case he was tired, but Max wanted to walk by himself. She always held his hand when they walked outside, but this morning Mrs. M was juggling the stroller and an umbrella as well as Max. They had just reached the bend in the road that turned into Fifty-Seventh Street when someone raced up behind Mrs. M, shoved her, and snatched Max.

The movement was so sudden and aggressive that Mrs. M fell to the ground. She screamed and so did Max, but just then a car pulled up behind them and slowed. The man who had Max opened the back door and threw himself and the boy into the back. The car sped off.

Everything happened so fast that Mrs. M didn't have time to catch the license plate. Not that it would help. It would take hours, if not days, to find the DMV record of the auto. Mrs. M raced home to call the police.

Lena didn't remember the ride in the squad car, but twenty minutes later, she was talking to two policemen in her living room. Officers were combing the area, they said; they were marshaling all their resources to find Max.

But they were at a disadvantage. They didn't know the make of the car—all Mrs. M could recall was a dark sedan. They didn't have a license plate either, or a solid description of the kidnapper. Still, they were canvassing neighbors, and cruisers were parked at Fifty-Seventh Street to stop and question motorists. They sent cops to the museum to interview the guards and staff. A photo of Max had been circulated and was being posted. No one wanted another Leopold and Loeb.

Lena listened as the officers explained, but their voices seemed to be muffled by a thick, hazy blanket. She felt distanced from the conversation, as though she didn't quite understand what they were saying. In a corner of her brain she knew she was in shock, but she had no idea how to deal with it. She sat on her sofa, hands folded politely in her lap, as if she were listening to a piano concerto.

FBI Agent Lanier, the same agent who'd come when Karl died, showed up thirty minutes later with an appropriately chagrined expression. Mrs. M went through her story again, shooting apologetic glances at Lena.

When Mrs. M finished, Lanier told Lena to stay at home and

near the phone. "The chances are good whoever has Max will make a ransom call before long."

"But I can't pay. I have no money." It was the first thing she'd said since Lanier arrived.

"They don't know that. They probably think Mrs. McNulty is a nanny or governess and you live in one of those big homes on Hyde Park Avenue. The two of them were perfect marks."

Lena made a sound that wasn't quite a sob. "I'm a secretary at the university. It's all I can do to put food on the table."

"You're working at Met Lab again, right?"

"Yes. The Physics Department."

Lanier nodded, as if he was confirming what he already knew, and changed the subject. He didn't press her about the work going on there, but Lena couldn't have told him if he had. She'd signed a strict confidentiality agreement when she went back. She could speak of it to no one, including the authorities.

Time seemed to stop that afternoon. After the police officers left, it was quiet except for the plunk of raindrops against the windows. Lena didn't move from her spot on the sofa. Agent Lanier stayed but didn't talk much. Around five he said he was going back to the office, but another detective would arrive. As he opened the door to leave, he gave her explicit instructions.

"When you get the call, call me immediately. They'll tell you not to, but you must. We'll be working in the background to get your boy back." He paused. "Mrs. Stern, there are good reasons to think he will be returned safely. More than one person was involved. Which means it was a conspiracy. They took him for a reason. Probably money. If it had been just one man, we'd be looking at a more ominous situation. Don't lose faith."

He left and closed the door softly. Faith? Lena had no faith.

Watching raindrops dribble sideways across a window, she knew, again, that she must have done something very wicked to warrant the punishments that had befallen her. Why had God chosen her?

Slowly she rose from the sofa and trudged into the kitchen. She took a tall glass from the cabinet and filled it with water. She drank about half, then examined the glass. She turned around and hurled the glass across the room. It smashed against the opposite wall and exploded, flinging shards of glass and water across the floor. The sound of shattering glass was oddly comforting.

CHAPTER 15

The telephone call came after Lanier left but before the police detective arrived. Lena had just finished cleaning up the broken glass, and the ring startled her. She raced to the phone, then hesitated. Why now? Who knew she would be alone at this precise moment?

"I assume the detective has left." It was a gruff male voice, but it was muffled, as if he were speaking through a towel or blanket.

"Who is this?"

"Someone you want to talk to. Is the babysitter gone?"

Mrs. M, still hysterical, had gone up to her apartment to try to calm down.

Someone had been watching her apartment. Lena started to tremble. "I—I'm alone," she stammered.

"Good. We have Max. He's fine. And we want to bring him back."

"Thank God. Please bring him right away."

"We will. But we want something in return."

Her stomach twisted. She bit her lip. "I have no money."

There was a laugh on the other end of the line. A laugh! "We know. In fact, we will help you change that."

"What—what are you saying?"

"We want to reimburse you for your pain and suffering. God knows you've had your share."

"How do you know that? Who are you? I want my son!"

"You will get him. But you must agree to our proposition."

"What proposition?"

"A man will be coming to your home in a few minutes. He will be wearing a policeman's uniform. But he is not an officer. You will let him in. Do you understand?"

"Yes, but—"

"Once you have agreed to the proposition, Max will be returned."

"Tonight? You'll bring him back tonight?"

"Yes. We have not harmed him. And we don't want to."

"What if I cannot accept the proposition? What if I refuse?"

"That would not be a good idea, Lena. For you or Max."

• • •

The man to whom Lena opened the door was unremarkable in every way. Average height, average weight, average thinning brown hair. Horn-rimmed glasses. His only distinguishing feature was a pair of oversized ears. Dressed in a cop's uniform, he had a badge pinned to his chest. If she'd been asked to describe him later, she wouldn't have been able to provide much.

He deposited himself on the sofa where she'd been sitting just a few minutes earlier. She picked up the baby blanket she'd been holding to remind her of Max's smell, and sat in the chair.

"Is Max all right? What have you done with him?"

He cleared his throat. "He is fine. But I only have a few minutes, Frau Stern, so here's what we want." He paused. "Information." He spoke with an unmistakable accent. It was German. From the South. Probably Bavaria. Erich, Ursula's husband, had a similar accent, and he was from Regensburg.

She folded her arms. "What information?" she said in German.

His eyes narrowed for a quick moment, and she saw in his expression that under the right circumstances he was probably capable of enormous cruelty. Despite the heat in the apartment, she shivered again. He must have realized his effect on her, because he unexpectedly bared his teeth in what she supposed was a smile.

"Information you come by on a daily basis," he answered in English.

She didn't reply at first. She was trying to process why he hadn't answered in German. Then she cast the thought aside. If that was what he wanted to do, what choice did she have? She wanted her son. "So you want me to spy at my job," she said in English.

The smile that wasn't really a smile widened. "They said you were a quick study."

"Who are you working for?" she asked, although she really didn't need to. It was clear. "You want me to spy for the Nazis?"

He didn't confirm it but didn't disagree.

"Why would I ever do that? After what you—they did to me? To my family? To my life? I'd rather die than help those—you monsters."

He nodded as if he wasn't surprised at her reaction. "I understand. But there is really only one point to consider. If you do not comply, you will never see your son again."

She stared at the man, then let her head sink into her hands. The tears that refused to come earlier now welled. Her life consisted of a series of events she could not control. Now there was one more.

The fake cop cleared his throat. "Frau Stern, we do not have much time. Another police officer will arrive soon."

Once more she was trapped. She had to play along. She breathed in the scent of the blanket. Without Max, life was not worth living. She hoped God would forgive her. Then she scoffed at the thought. There was no God. At least for her. That was abundantly clear. She looked over, blinking through her tears.

"What is it you want me to do?"

"We want you to bring us whatever you come across in your daily work. Letters, files, theoretical analyses, observations. Photos of the lab, if you can. It is clear America is committed to building an atomic weapon, and we know there are several paths to that end. We know Chicago is working on one option. We need to know what your scientists know. As soon as they know it. You will provide it."

"But what happens if they find out?" she asked. "Will you help me escape? Find someplace for Max and me to disappear to?"

The man cleared his throat. "We understand this will not be easy. Or risk-free. It is quite possible someone at some point will suspect what you are doing."

The answer was no, she thought. They would do nothing if she was unmasked. She was on her own.

"That is why we are willing to compensate you. Generously," he went on. "We will pay you two hundred dollars a month."

Her mouth opened. It was a fortune. Her money problems

would disappear. "We know you have had financial problems since the untimely death of your husband."

Untimely? What did that mean, "untimely"? She peered at him, but his expression remained flat. Then he cocked his head.

"A word of warning, Lena. Do not think you can get away from us. We are watching you. We know every step that you take. Once you start down this road, there is no going back."

Lena hated this man and his words. But she couldn't go to the authorities. She was a German herself. A refugee. And although she was now a US citizen, every German was suspect these days. They might even decide she was already spying. Then what would happen to her and Max? She couldn't risk it. She was trapped.

The man looked at his watch. "I must leave." He cleared his throat. "But there is one other matter. You will need to learn tradecraft."

"What does that mean, 'tradecraft'?"

"There are many ways to retrieve and exchange information. You will learn the basic techniques. I will teach you."

"You're going to teach me how to be a spy!"

"I wouldn't call it that."

"What would you call it?" She knew she sounded irritated. She wanted him to get that.

"Methods to manage your risk. And ours." He hesitated. "So. What is your answer?"

She stared and took a deep breath, hoping it would make him uncomfortable. "You give me no choice."

The man pulled out an envelope from his jacket pocket. He opened it and counted out ten twenty-dollar bills, which he laid on the coffee table.

Her mouth fell open again.

"You need not see me out. We start training tomorrow. You will find a note in your mailbox with the meeting time and location."

Lena picked up the money. "Since we are to be working together, what is your name?"

"You may call me Hans."

She nodded. "What about Max, Hans?"

He rose from the sofa. "Your son will be dropped off shortly."

The promise was kept. Ten minutes later, the buzzer rang. Lena raced down the steps. As she opened the front door, a car pulled away, leaving Max standing on the curb. He held a balloon in one hand and a small cherry lollipop in the other. His lips were stained red, as if he'd been sucking on it for hours.

"Hello, Mama." He grinned.

She closed her arms around him. She wished she could grab Max and run away. But where would she go? She had no money, and the only people she knew in Chicago were her aunt Ursula and Erich. As a German immigrant, she couldn't go to the authorities—they would never believe her, despite the kidnapping. They'd think she was making it up, a fantasy brought about by grief over her dead husband. And if this Hans fellow found out, she and Max would be in mortal danger. She was trapped.

CHAPTER 16

"Americans are suspicious of everything," Hans told Lena a week later. "But they must not be suspicious of you."

They were walking down State Street in the Loop on a crisp Saturday morning in April. It was still early, and the sun slanted through the buildings and bounced off shop windows in a cheerful display of light. "You must always be aware of your surroundings, the environment, and the people. Be alert for someone or something that could compromise your security. It might be quite small and inconsequential, and it will probably be the one thing that doesn't belong." He stopped. "For example, what color was the dress of the woman who just passed us?"

Hans had a fast stride, and Lena was concentrating on keeping pace with him. She had no idea about the dress. "I don't know," she said.

"Turn around."

She did. The dress was powder blue. She turned back.

"What about her shoes?"

Lena's spirits sank. It was one thing to make sure she didn't bump into people as they hurried down the street. It was quite another to remember what shoes they were wearing.

"They were black," he said. "Was she wearing perfume?"

Lena shrugged.

As if reading her mind, he went on. "She was. But do not worry. It will come. The point is, you must not do anything to raise an alarm . . . to make people think their security is at stake. But *your* security is critical. If it seems too much of a risk, if you think someone is tailing you, abort the mission. Figure out how to accomplish it a different way."

Hans had been training Lena for five days. Despite the fact that it was hard to leave Max, she had worked with Hans every evening after work and now today. He had divided her education into subjects. Today was surveillance. He was teaching her how to tell if she was being followed, and if so, how to lose the tail. He was also showing her how to tail someone else, although he admitted she likely wouldn't have much use for that skill. Her primary activity was simply to supply information about the research and development going on at Met Lab. Still, he said, she should be familiar with basic techniques.

They had already discussed communication. She would buy a flowerpot for her windowsill, he said, and move it from one side to the other to signal a meet or indicate something was in the dead drop. He also taught her to watch for signals from him. How to follow chalk marks, bottle caps, orange peels, or tacks affixed to telephone poles. He pointed out two dead drops, both within a block of her apartment, where she would leave rolls of film and documents. She was surprised she'd never noticed them before; then again, that was the point. He taught her how to spot a classified ad in the newspaper that was really a coded message and how to decrypt it. Her brain was swimming.

"And those are just the simple methods," he reminded her.

The next area they needed to discuss, he said, as they continued down State, was tools. "You will clearly need a camera so you can take pictures of the setup as well as documents."

Lena frowned. "But how—"

He cut her off. "Of course we would prefer the actual documents, but we know in your case that will not be possible. Photos will suffice. You will leave a roll of film in the dead drop every time you have something."

"What if I'm not able to take photos?"

"You will find a way. Work late. Come in early."

"Everyone already does."

"Then go in earlier. Stay later. Go in on a weekend."

"And how am I supposed to get the film out of the office?"

He waved a hand. "Your purse. A briefcase. You will figure it out."

"I don't carry a briefcase. It would look pretentious if I began."

"Improvise. A grocery bag. Your coat pockets. Here." He stopped walking, pulled out his wallet, and peeled off a twenty. "Go into Marshall Field's and buy a new bag. A big one."

Lena didn't miss a beat. "And the camera?"

He laughed. "You learn quickly. We will supply it. Go into the store. I will wait."

They were standing under the clock at State and Randolph. She headed toward the store entrance. Then she turned around and came back. "What about a gun?"

"A gun? For you?"

She nodded.

"No gun."

She spun around and went into Field's.

CHAPTER 17

Much to Lena's chagrin, Agent Lanier came around twice after the incident. He claimed he couldn't figure out who had taken and then returned Max with no questions asked.

Hans had told Lena what to say. "I have no idea," she recited. "What do you think?"

"Like I said, I don't know. I really thought it was a ransom case."

"Agent Lanier." She smiled. "Perhaps you did a better job than you thought. Perhaps the people who took him knew they couldn't get away with it." She barreled on. "I'm just grateful to have him back. I never want to go through that again. Especially so soon after my husband's death." She swallowed and bit her lip, as if she was trying to suppress tears.

He scratched his cheek. "Yeah, that is a factor. I can't help but wonder whether the two incidents are related."

Lena went pale.

"Oh, come on, Mrs. Stern. Surely the same thought has crossed your mind."

She didn't answer for a moment. "Of course it has. But how? For what purpose?"

He cocked his head. "I was hoping you could tell me."

"You must remember I lost my parents. My homeland. My husband. And then I almost lost my son." She shook her head. "Agent Lanier, I cannot survive another loss."

After a long moment, he nodded. "I understand. I'll leave you in peace. But I want to—"

"Yes?"

"I think we know each other well enough to use first names, don't you? I'm Peter. But everyone calls me Pete."

Lena smiled. "Lena."

"Here's my card. If you ever need anything, feel free to call."

• • •

Hans fabricated a story to tell the people at Met Lab about Max. Lena was to say he had not been kidnapped after all. He had simply wandered off from Mrs. M and got lost. He'd been found by a Good Samaritan and returned a few hours later. Everyone seemed to accept it, which made Lena feel guilty. Compton had gone out of his way to rehire her after Karl died. Adjusted her schedule so she could be with Max. Even kept on Sonia, the other secretary, to share the load. And the way she repaid him? Lies and duplicity.

Indeed, her stomach pitched every time she thought about what she was doing. But when the money arrived promptly each week in fifty-dollar increments, it made a difference. She began to pay off the grocer's bill. For the first time since Karl died, she could afford the rent, and she even had a little extra to lavish on Max. She came to depend on the money and started to see her job through a different lens. Everything she handled or saw could be measured by whether she could snap photos of it, and how much she was being paid to do so.

It wasn't difficult to monitor the goings-on at the lab. Major events seemed to occur every day. Fermi was now working in Chicago along with Glenn Seaborg and Leo Szilard, and someone named Bush was the liaison between Compton and the president.

The first document she photographed was a letter from Bush to Compton about the Army Corps of Engineers, which had been tasked with building whatever weapon was created. Several officers were named as key contacts, and she knew Hans and his people would want to know who they were. Hans had given her a tiny camera called a Minox. About the size and shape of a small comb, it fit easily in her bag or pocket and was perfect for photographing documents. It had been designed by a German, he said.

A few days later, on a rain-soaked afternoon that made Lena glad she was inside, she told Sonia that she would stay until it stopped. She'd forgotten to bring her umbrella. "You know how unpredictable Chicago weather is."

"Why don't you take mine?" Sonia said. "My sister is coming to pick me up. I'll share hers."

Lena's stomach clenched, and her pulse sped up. "Oh no. I have work to do, anyway."

Sonia glanced over and smiled. "Well, then, take it when you leave. I know you'll bring it back."

Lena bit her lip. "Thank you," she managed. She hoped she sounded casual, but her insides were churning. Had she sounded ungrateful? Too dismissive? Would Sonia suspect something? Some spy, she thought. Her first assignment and she was already worried about exposure. Maybe she should just go to Compton and confess. How could she live with this kind of stress every time she chatted with a colleague? If she did confess, though, what would Hans and his people do to Max? As long as they were around, her son would never be free from their clutches, whoever "they" were. And she was sure "they" were Nazis. She kept her mouth shut.

It wasn't until nine that evening that she was finally alone in the office. Everything was quiet, except for the buzz of the fluorescent lights and the trickle of rain on the windows. She waited another minute, then went to the filing cabinets that stood behind her and Sonia's desks. They were locked, but she and Sonia had keys. She unlocked the nearest cabinet and pulled out the top drawer. The files were arranged chronologically, and the letter Bush had written to Compton was in front. She laid the paper on top of the cabinet, then thought better of it and brought it back to her desk.

Slipping the Minox out of her bag, she paused, listening for any change in the ambient sound. Nothing. But she could smell the fear on herself, and her hands shook so much she had to take half a dozen photos of the letter. When she was finished, she dropped the camera into her bag, hurriedly put the letter back, and relocked the cabinet. She grabbed her bag and rushed out.

She was almost home, making record time despite the rain, when she realized she'd left Sonia's umbrella at the office. An icicle of fear slid around her stomach. What should she do? She couldn't lie and say the rain had stopped; it was still coming down at a steady rate. But if she didn't bring it in tomorrow, Sonia might suspect something. Better to be safe. She trudged back to the department to fetch the umbrella, then retraced her way home.

Inside the front hall she shook out the umbrella and practically ran up the stairs to her apartment. Max was fast asleep, and Mrs. M was snoring in the living room. Lena tiptoed further into her son's room and kissed him on the forehead. It took thirty minutes for her breathing to return to normal.

CHAPTER 18

After a month it was easier. There were even times when Lena felt justified in her behavior. She had found a way to strike back at the events that had defined her life. She was no longer at the whim of fate. She was taking action. In control. She enjoyed the money, too. In fact, taking money from the Nazis gave her a perverse sense of satisfaction. She bought new clothes for herself and Max and put a new sofa and easy chair for the living room on layaway.

One morning she wore a new navy blue dress with white polka dots and a huge bow to work. When Sonia caught sight of her, she whistled. "Well, hi-de-ho! Aren't you the pretty picture!" She cocked her head. "You have a new boyfriend or something?"

Lena felt her cheeks get hot. "Of course not. It has only been five months since Karl died."

Sonia looked her over. "Well, then, I guess I'd better ask Compton for the same raise you got," she said.

Lena made a mental note not to wear new clothes to the office again. And although part of her was secretly proud of her newfound ability to provide for herself and Max, part of her, too, was ashamed at the source of the money.

The worst times were when she ran into Compton. Her pulse would speed up; her cheeks grew hot. She was sure he could see straight through her and was waiting to confront her. She imagined what Hester Prynne must have felt like wearing that scarlet letter across her chest. On those days she'd rush home from work, clasp Max in her arms, and cry.

• • •

Hans didn't signal for a meeting until June. She was on her way to work, the morning bright and full of the promise of summer. June usually reminded Lena of her wedding day, but today, tears didn't spring to her eyes. Indeed, this was new, this sense of satisfaction. Was this what it was like to feel like she belonged? To own a tiny piece of the American dream? Despite the war, despite what was happening in Europe, despite everything, she had resources. Perhaps she could look the other way, pretend the nefarious work she was doing didn't exist.

She was so wrapped up in this new thought, turning it this way and that in her mind, that she almost missed the orange peel on the corner of Fifty-Seventh and Kimbark. As soon as she spotted it, she squeezed her eyes shut. She couldn't pretend. As much as she wanted to imagine, this wasn't make-believe.

At lunch she told Sonia she was going out for a walk and headed toward the Museum of Science and Industry. She wandered around the main floor, admiring the high ceilings and massive columns of the former Palace of Fine Arts. Julius Rosenwald, the chairman of Sears, Roebuck and Company, got the idea for the museum after visiting a similar place in Munich thirty years earlier with his son. The Rosenwalds held a special place in Lena's heart. Rosenwald's son, William, organized an effort in the mid-1930s to help Jews in Nazi Germany emigrate to the US. Some people *did* do the right thing, she mused. Of course, they had the money and means.

She was thinking about how life could surprise you with its decency when Hans appeared at her side. He took her arm, as if they were lovers about to steal a precious hour together. They strolled to an area where workmen were building a miniature train and village that would fill an entire wing. The exhibit was to open at Christmas.

"You are well, Lena?" Hans asked.

"Very. And you?" She answered cautiously.

"I am fine." A small smile crossed his face. "So. We have a new priority for you."

She raised her eyebrows.

"We know that American scientists are trying to build chain-reacting 'piles' to produce plutonium, and then extract it from the irradiated uranium so they can build an atomic bomb. We want you to focus on the pile and the tests that are planned in it."

She tried to hide her surprise. "How do you know this?"

"Come, Lena. You must realize you are not our only asset." He laughed. "Although you are certainly the most attractive."

Lena blew out a breath.

"We know that a group headed by Compton's chief engineer, Thomas Moore, began designing the pile under the west stands of Stagg Field."

"Tell me, Hans, who is 'we'? Haven't I proven myself enough to tell me about the others in your group?"

Hans raised a finger to his lips. "We need the plans for the pile."

She hesitated. Then: "I know I have made a pact with the devil, but I need more specifics. It will help me tailor what I give you."

"Lena, let's keep to the subject at hand. We need to find out how they are building the pile."

"But that is impossible. I am not allowed anywhere near it."

"There must be a blueprint."

"If there is, neither Sonia nor I have high enough clearances to see it."

"Then you'll have to think of a way to get the information."

"How? I can't break in. There are guards there all night."

Hans clasped his free hand over hers. "You're a resourceful woman. You will find a way."

CHAPTER 19

Lena's mood deteriorated after the meet with Hans. She was dirty, scheming, worse than a tease. In fact, she was nothing more than a whore for the Nazis—supplying information rather than sex. But this was her lot. She had agreed to it. And so over the next few days she studied the scientists at the Met Lab, particularly the younger ones, wondering who would become her unwitting accomplice.

She finally settled on Irving Mandell, a shy, self-effacing young man from the South Side who had stayed at the university after earning his PhD. He worked on the pile, and she knew he held the highest clearance possible. He was skinny and tall, with curly black hair that resembled a messy bird's nest and an acne-scarred face. His eyes were large and soulful, but he wore a perpetually timid expression.

She made sure she was at her desk when he came and went each day and started with cheery "good mornings" and "good nights." That led to brief conversations and lots of smiles on her part. At one point, two weeks later, after one conversation, she ran to the ladies' room, afraid she was going to vomit. She didn't recognize herself. What had she become?

Sonia followed her in with a worried frown. "You're as white as Casper's ghost. What's wrong?"

Lena shook her head.

Sonia's eyes narrowed. That was not a good sign. Lena would have to be more careful.

Two weeks after that, her efforts paid off. She and Irving had shared coffee on one occasion and lunch on another, and this evening they'd met for a beer at the restaurant she and Karl used to frequent. Lena always kept the conversation focused on physics and work. "I've always wanted to understand better," she said. "But I never had the chance to study. You know, coming from Germany when I did . . ." She let her voice trail off.

Irving nodded earnestly. Although he wasn't aware of it, he had played his part perfectly. He was by turns the eager scholar, the wise teacher, the ardent suitor. Lena was sure no woman had ever paid him this much attention, and she felt a stab of guilt every time she flashed him a smile or brushed his hand with her fingers, as she did now.

He launched into an explanation of how plutonium could theoretically be separated from irradiated uranium.

"Is that what you're doing in the pile?"

"That's part of it. You see, if we can successfully do that, we can then manufacture as much as we need. And then . . ." He frowned. "You know, I'm not supposed to talk about it with anyone. Including coworkers."

She looked over. "Of course you're not. I'm sorry. I don't mean to . . ." She swallowed.

"What?" he asked.

She lifted a shoulder, then shook her head. "Nothing."

His expression softened. "What is it, Lena?"

"I—I would love to see the pile. Is it safe to go in?"

"Oh yes."

"No chance of people getting irradiated, is there?"

"None whatsoever." He laughed. "Tell me, Lena, why is the pile so important?"

She looked down. "It's—it's just that we—you and I and all the others—will be a part of history. What you are doing will change the world forever."

He folded his arms.

"I—guess I just wanted to share a tiny little part of it. I long to see it. Even just for a few seconds." She flashed him a sad smile. "Still, I understand. You cannot compromise security."

Irving let out a sigh. He looked left, then right, as if he thought someone might be watching. "I would love to show it to you," he said. "But I can't take the chance."

Lena nodded, as if resigned to his decision. "Let's talk about something else, shall we?" She glanced at her watch. "Oh dear, it's after seven. I really must get home. Max and Mrs. M will wonder what has become of me."

Irving leaned over the table and kissed her cheek. She brushed his cheek with her fingers. "You are the best thing that's ever happened to me," he said.

"You don't mind that I'm an old woman?" she teased. She was three years older.

"Are you kidding? The rest of the guys are jealous."

"You've told them about us?" She tried to make herself blush. "Oh no."

"Was I wrong?" A worried frown came over him.

She didn't reply for a moment. Then she smiled prettily. "I—I guess not."

They both rose from the table. He clasped her hand in his. "Come. I will walk you home."

"You do not have to."

"I know."

But outside the restaurant he turned west, not east, which was the way to Lena's apartment. She pulled on his arm. "We should be going the other way, Irving."

He took her hand again. "Where we're going you must never speak of. Ever. Do you understand?"

Her stomach flipped. "I understand," she whispered. "It never happened."

They walked the few blocks toward Stagg Field.

CHAPTER 20

They arrived at the stadium and walked around to the western corner. The evening was hot and humid; within minutes, sweat ringed Lena's neck. She wiped a handkerchief across her brow.

"Stay here," Irving said and ducked inside.

Lena gazed at the field's brick exterior, much of it covered by ivy. At each corner, a turret rose above the structure as if it was a well-guarded castle. Windows above the first floor were shaded with awnings, while bars covered the windows at ground level. If she walked through the gate, she would eventually find herself in the middle of the field, the seats in the open like the bleachers at Wrigley.

The lack of protection made for icy football games, and she'd never attended one. She never understood why Americans thought a group of burly young men attacking and hurling one another to the ground was sporting. It was barbaric, not at all like the civilized football—or soccer, as they called it in the US—she'd known in Europe.

Irving came back out, jogged across the street, and reached for her hand. "Come quickly." He sounded out of breath.

"Are you sure?"

He reached down and kissed her.

She returned it. "You will not get into trouble?"

"If I do"—he smiled—"it will have been worth it."

They walked through the entrance, down a flight of stairs, and around a corner to a closed door. There was no one outside.

"Where's the guard?"

Irving raised his palm in a gesture that said to keep quiet. Then he yanked his thumb behind him. Lena spun around but didn't see anyone. Irving whispered, "He just passed by. We only have a minute."

She nodded and watched him fish a key out of his pocket. Unlocking the door with one hand, he ushered her inside with the other.

Lena wasn't sure what she'd expected. From the memos and letters she'd seen, she knew the pile contained 771,000 pounds of graphite, 80,590 pounds of uranium oxide, and 12,400 pounds of uranium metal. It cost one million dollars to build. The pile was described as a flattened ellipsoid, constructed on the lattice principle, with graphite as a moderator, and lumps of metal or oxide. They were the reacting units and were spaced through the graphite to form the lattice. Instruments situated at various points in the pile or near it indicated the neutron intensity, and movable strips of absorbing material served as controls.

But that was the abstract definition. What she saw was a room, once a squash court, about twenty-five feet wide, its ceiling twenty feet high. At one end was a contraption that rose from floor to ceiling. Most of it was built out of bricks, with a brick wall in the center and what looked like terraced "piles" of bricks above it, each recessed more than the pile below. The ceiling above the pile looked like it was made out of cushions, although Lena knew that wasn't the case. Behind the bricks, she knew from the letters she'd typed, were the tons of graphite, uranium oxide, and uranium metal.

Something resembling a long faucet protruded from the lowest pile, but again, Lena didn't know if water came out of it. A ladder leaned against the brick wall. To the right of the contraption was a set of stairs; on the other side was a thick curtain that might have been lead, which separated the pile from the rest of the room. Adjacent to that was a series of cubicles about twelve feet high, each containing odd-looking pieces of equipment, none of which she could identify.

Irving watched her gaze at the contraption with wide-eyed amazement. "So what do you think?"

"I—I don't know. I didn't know what to expect. It looks rather benign, actually. What do you call it? I mean, besides Pile Number One? Is it going to be a bomb?"

"This is a nuclear reactor. It's very different from a bomb," he said with a touch of pride.

Lena furrowed her brow. "Then why build it? I mean, what does it do?"

"It would take a semester to explain it to you," he said, "but basically, a bomb requires a huge amount of fissionable material. So that's what we're trying to do—create a lot of fissionable material quickly."

"How do you do that?" she asked, becoming interested in spite of herself.

"That's what we're working out. We think it's by creating a

chain reaction that will essentially 'cook' uranium and produce energy. While it's cooking, it forms plutonium, which we need for the bomb. Once it's cooled, we will try to separate the plutonium from the uranium. But the plutonium will be highly radioactive, so we have to build machines that can do all this by remote control."

"I had no idea."

Irving grinned. "Yes. But you see, there are other scientists around the country experimenting with other materials. It's almost a race to see which team produces results first. Of course, we think it will be us," Irving said with a hint of pride.

The sound of footsteps clattered outside the door to the reactor room. Irving's eyes went wide. "The guard is coming back. We have to get out." He grabbed her arm, and they sprinted to the stairs in the corner of the room. "Follow me."

• • •

Back home twenty minutes later, after a long good-night kiss, Lena drew a sketch of the reactor. She searched her memory to make sure she included all the details. She was nearly finished when the phone rang.

"Lena? It's Ursula."

"Hello. Are you all right? Is Erich?"

"We're fine, but I have some bad news."

Lena stiffened.

"We received a letter from friends back in Berlin. They said your parents were rounded up last year and resettled in the East."

Lena squeezed her eyes shut. "Where?"

"Who knows? The rumors are somewhere in Poland."

Lena nodded to herself. She'd gone to an occasional service at

KAM Isaiah Israel, where the rabbi told congregants what was really happening to the Jews in Europe.

Ursula paused. "I think you need to prepare yourself, *Liebchen*. You have no doubt heard about the Nazis' Final Solution. There is little doubt about their future. I am so sorry."

Lena didn't reply for a moment. "I understand. Thank you, Ursula." She replaced the receiver quietly, as if any additional sound would break the telephone into pieces.

She went back to her sketch of the pile. She wanted to tear it up, tell Hans she hadn't been able to complete the mission. Then she had a better idea. She stared at the drawing. She couldn't change it too much; Hans had told her she wasn't their only asset. Still, she was probably the only asset who'd actually been inside the pile. She altered the sketch just enough, removing the faucet, the "booths" on the side of the pile, and the cushiony material on the ceiling.

• • •

The next morning on her way to work, she sought out a crevice in a waist-high stone wall on Dorchester. It was the primary dead drop for her rolls of film, but the sketch, which she'd slipped into a white envelope, was too large for the space, and the envelope was clearly visible. Flicking an imaginary spot off her jacket, she glanced in both directions. No one was coming. She casually dropped the envelope back in her purse and returned home. She opened the curtains in the living room, raised the window, and moved the flowerpot filled with pansies to the other side of the sill.

Hans dropped by her apartment after work. The thick summer sun was still so punishing that even the shadows held no relief. Rings of sweat stained Lena's blouse under her armpits, but when

Hans arrived, he was wearing a wool jacket. She was about to ask why he was torturing himself, but when she watched him tuck the envelope into his inside pocket, she understood.

The next day as she walked to work, she started to think about breaking it off with Irving. Her job was done, but, of course, Irving didn't know she'd been using him, and he'd summoned up all his courage and asked her out to the movies. She'd politely declined, claiming she needed to spend more time with Max, which was true. Her son was the love of her life. Wasn't that why she was doing this in the first place? She'd just have to tell Irving she wasn't ready for a relationship—the mourning period for Jews usually lasted a year anyway. She was practicing what to tell him when a strange sensation came over her.

Someone was following her.

She turned around and saw a black sedan crawling along Fifty-Seventh Street a few yards behind her. Her gaze went to the license plate, which was supposed to be bolted to the fender, but there was none. Adrenaline flooded through her, and every sense went on alert. She tried to remember what Hans had told her about losing a tail. Fortunately, an alley lay just ahead. She ducked into it, then spun around to get a look at the car and driver. The driver, a man, was wearing a straw boater and sunglasses, which effectively disguised his face. Yet there was something familiar about him. The set of his head. The shape of his face. Still, she couldn't place him. She stared after the sedan, but it turned right at the next corner and disappeared.

CHAPTER 21

Chicago, August-September 1942

In August some of the physicists at Met Lab isolated a microscopic amount of plutonium. It was a major development; the entire department buzzed with the news. This meant that it *was* possible to separate plutonium from uranium and thus produce a supply of it for the bomb. Met Lab was on the right track. In the meantime, Enrico Fermi and his team continued with experiments that would produce a chain reaction in the pile.

Lena fed the information to Hans. He'd been uncharacteristically overjoyed with her sketch of the pile, and he seemed fascinated by every new development. She also passed him the news that construction of the bomb and its materials would not be in Chicago. Production would relocate to the Clinch River in Tennessee and would be turned over to a private firm reporting to the army. An experimental pile would be built in the Argonne Forest Preserve just outside Chicago, but the Met

Lab scientists were just that, scientists and researchers, not facility operators. Compton had wanted to keep everything at the university, she told Hans, but he was overruled. People were fearful of an accident in such a heavily populated area.

In September, the army appointed Colonel Leslie R. Groves to head the production effort, which was now called the Manhattan Project. Groves, a former West Pointer with the Army Corps of Engineers, had supervised the construction of the Pentagon building in Washington. When Groves took command, he made it clear that by the end of the year, a decision would be made as to which process would be used to produce a bomb.

Lena dutifully reported the news to Hans. Occasionally Hans would meet her in a black Ford, and they'd drive around the South Side. Other times they met in a coffee shop, always a different one. This time he drove to a diner, where they sat at the counter. A fresh-faced boy with a peaked white cap took their order of iced tea for Lena, a chocolate milk shake for Hans. Leaning her elbows on the counter, Lena watched the boy make the milk shake.

"Do you have another car, a black sedan of some sort?" she asked.

Hans frowned. It took him a moment to reply. He shook his head. "No. Why?"

"Someone was following me in a black car. I did not know the make."

"When?"

"Perhaps a month or so ago."

"And you remember that far back?"

"I do. It was—unnerving."

"Where was it?"

"On Fifty-Seventh Street. In the morning. I was on my way to work."

Hans arched his eyebrows. "Did you see who it was?"

She shook her head. "He was wearing sunglasses and a boater."

Hans splayed his hands on the counter. "I have no idea."

Lena looked over. "The man looked familiar. But I couldn't place him."

Hans shrugged. "Perhaps he just wanted to follow an attractive woman." He smiled, but it looked forced.

The boy behind the counter brought their drinks. Lena reached for a straw and sipped her tea. Hans hadn't made the slightest move toward her in the months they'd been working together. He'd been totally professional, although he had to know she'd been using her womanly charms on Irving. For a moment she wondered why he kept her at a distance, especially when he told her more than once how attractive she was. Then she decided it was better this way. Not only was he a Nazi; he would be another thing to worry about.

CHAPTER 22

Chicago, September 1942

Lena was at work one evening in late September. The door to the department was closed, but a breeze with just a hint of fall wafted through a window. She was glad summer was over; the heat and humidity had seemed particularly harsh this year. She'd just finished photographing the latest batch of letters and documents and was putting the originals back into the file cabinet when she felt a draft. She spun around.

A man in an army uniform stood at the door to the department, his gaze locked on her. The stripes on his shoulders said he was an officer. He had short bristly gray hair and pale blue eyes that were a touch rheumy. Frown lines etched his forehead. He'd once been fit, she thought, but a large belly indicated those days were over. In the short sleeves of his summer uniform, his arms and the backs of his hands were covered with heavy dark hair, which gave him a slightly simian look.

Lena froze. How long had he been there? Why hadn't she heard the door open? What had he seen? Panic crawled up her spine. Her arms and legs felt like they had suddenly detached from her body.

The man folded his arms. "And just what are you doing, young lady?"

The blood left her head in a rush. She wanted to look down to see if her hands were shaking but she didn't dare. This was it. She had been caught. Then she recalled one of Hans's rules of tradecraft. If she was ever cornered or caught, the best defense was a good offense. She'd told Hans at the time she didn't know if she could. He'd chuckled and said, "You will. You'll see."

Now she realized he was right. There was no other option. She drew herself up, not sure where her courage was coming from. "I should be asking the same of you."

The officer's brows shot up. "Do you know who I am?"

Lena mustered what she hoped was an intimidating scowl. "I have no idea. So I will call security. This is a protected facility." She started toward the telephone on her desk.

He took a step forward. "I am Colonel Charles Collins."

Lena continued to her desk and slipped behind it. Her purse was on the floor, and as she got to it, she unobtrusively kicked it further under the desk. Then she lifted her gaze, as if she'd just made the connection. "Collins? You were here a few years ago."

"I was. And now I'm back." His expression bordered on arrogance. "Who are you?"

She eyed him warily. A wave of trepidation rolled through her, but she was damned if she'd let him see it. "The department is closed, Colonel. In fact, I am obligated to report your unauthorized visit. How did you get this far? Our security is first-rate."

"Whoever you are, you clearly do not know my position."

"And you do not know mine." Lena was amazed at herself. Where had she acquired this steely resolve? She opened her drawer, took out paper and pen, and wrote his name down. "A report will be filed tomorrow morning."

"And to whom do you think the reports go?"

She looked him up and down, wondering if he could smell the fear on her.

"I am in charge of security. My job is to ensure there are no breaches at the Met Lab. Now. You either tell me who you are or I will have you detained."

Lena wasn't sure whether she believed him. If he really was the head of security, wouldn't he know who she was? She'd been working there for the past nine months. Still, in case he somehow didn't know and was telling the truth, she answered. "I am Lena Stern, one of the secretaries for the department." She hesitated. "And if what you are saying is true, why was I not told about you?" It felt like a bird was fluttering inside her stomach.

"Obviously your security clearance level is not high enough," he said.

The stress coupled with his self-importance made her want to let out a nervous laugh. She pressed her lips together so she wouldn't.

"Why are you here?" he repeated.

She parried the question. "If you are who you say you are, you would know."

He stared at her, his face reddening.

"There is so much work these days that I occasionally stay late to catch up." She bent down and reached for her purse, hoping he wouldn't spot the Minox lying on top. "But now, if you'll excuse me, Colonel"—she snapped the clasp of her purse shut—"I am going home."

She felt his eyes on her back as she walked out the door.

CHAPTER 23

Collins became a ubiquitous, unwanted presence in the department. He was intrusive, especially to those below his rank, which was almost everyone, since most of the scientists were civilians. But the army had been put back in charge of the Manhattan Project, and Collins was free to meddle. Every day he demanded clearances, records, documents, and memos, disrupting both Lena's and Sonia's workloads. They understood the importance of security, but Collins used it as a cudgel to force his way into situations. The only person who could control him was Compton, but he was preoccupied by meetings with top army and government officials and wasn't around much. Most of the staff came to loathe Collins.

Because of him, Lena told Hans she'd have to slow down for a while. It was too risky. Hans agreed. Lena was happy to leave work at a reasonable time for a change, and spent more time with Max. He was just three now, and a curious child. He asked questions all the time, and Lena found herself studying how birds flew, how clouds formed, and why leaves turned colors.

Meanwhile Irving continued to be worrisome. Lena hadn't had the heart to tell him they were through. Still, she did cut down on the time she spent with him, and she could tell he was growing frustrated. She worried about how he'd react when she told him it was over.

• • •

The crisis came in October. Lena had just put Max down for the night when the buzzer sounded. She pressed the intercom button, and a crisp voice said, "This is Colonel Collins."

Lena's knees buckled. Why was he here? Had he discovered proof of her treason? Was this the knock on her door in the middle of the night? She feared the worst. Still, she'd learned to be on the offense with him. "Colonel," she said sharply. "It's late. I'm just about to retire for the night."

He cleared his throat. "I have urgent business to discuss."

Her throat closed up. What should she do? His voice cut in. "Please, Mrs. Stern."

She drew back. He sounded almost polite. Could it possibly be about something other than her espionage? She took a breath and buzzed him in.

When she opened the door, she saw he was still in uniform, but it was wrinkled and creased as if he'd been rolling around on the floor. His face was pale as well. Normally, he had a too-ruddy look. She smelled alcohol on him.

"Thank you for seeing me," he said.

She gave him a cautious nod. "Come in, Colonel. But please keep your voice down. My son is asleep."

He stepped in and looked around. Lena's natural civility kicked in.

"Would you like a glass of water?"

"You got anything stronger?"

Surprised at the request, she stammered, "I—I—might." She went into the kitchen and rummaged through a cabinet. Irving had brought over some whiskey a few months earlier. She found it behind the canisters of flour and sugar. The bottle was nearly full. About to ask him how he took it, she turned around and suddenly started. Collins was standing in the doorway to the kitchen. She hadn't heard him approach. She jumped back. This is it, she thought. I am *gefickt*.

He held up his hand. "I'm sorry. I didn't mean to frighten you."

She let out a breath, trying to suppress her fear. "How—how do you take it? The whiskey, I mean?"

"Straight. Just a glass."

She got one out, filled it halfway, and handed it to him. They headed back to the living room. Lena sat in the chair, leaving him the sofa. She laced her hands together.

He sat down and took a long pull on the drink.

"What's so important, Colonel?" She tried to keep the edge out of her voice, but she was still nervous.

"I have a proposition for you."

Her eyebrows went up. If this was a confrontation, it was a strange way to begin. She sat up straighter.

"I know you are seeing one of the physicists in the department." She stiffened.

"Irving Mandell. Don't deny it. Several sources have confirmed it."

"Colonel," Lena said in a cool voice. "You know how tongues

wag and rumors begin. Usually they are greatly exaggerated. I lost my husband ten months ago. I am still in mourning."

"Are you saying it isn't true, Mrs. Stern?"

Lena couldn't resist. "It is not. But even if it was, what business is it of yours?"

"Mandell's business is very much my business, Mrs. Stern. We believe"—he cleared his throat—"that he is spying for a foreign government."

Lena froze. Irving? A spy? She sagged against the chair. How had they come to that conclusion? Or was this a trap? Was Collins accusing Irving, hoping that Lena would defend him and blurt out the truth? She had to be careful.

"That is impossible," she finally said. "Irving is one of the most loyal, patriotic people I know." She paused. "What makes you believe he isn't?"

"You know I can't divulge that. It's classified."

Of course it was, she thought. In some ways, with his visits after dark, his innuendo and interrogation techniques, this American was not so different from a Nazi. But what about the substance of his remarks? It was the pile, she decided. Someone knew she and Irving had been there. But why would he single out Irving and not her too?

"Mrs. Stern." He took another long drink. "You can deny it all you want, but I know the two of you are seeing each other. I have photos of you together. At a restaurant just off campus."

Stunned, Lena sat up straight. "You've been following us? And you have photos?" Her voice rose an octave. She was unsure whether to be terrified or furious.

Collins raised a finger to his lips. "You might want to lower your voice. Didn't you say your son was sleeping?" His mouth curled into a tiny smile of triumph.

Lena went mute. All she could do was glare.

He pointed his finger. "You see, Mrs. Stern, you're right about one thing. I don't care about the nature of your relationship. If the two of you are fucking like rabbits, that's your choice. What I do care about is the security of the Met Lab. And for that, I need your help."

Lena kept her mouth shut. She was afraid even to blink, for fear she would reveal something she shouldn't.

"In fact, I want you to keep your courtship going. See him as much as you can. Deepen your relationship." He couldn't resist a smile. "On one condition, of course. You will report back to me. Let me know everything he is doing. At work and at play. I need evidence."

"You want me to spy on my coworker."

"Plural," he said.

"What are you talking about?"

"Mandell is number one on my list. But there are others. I want you to be my eyes and ears when I'm not around. Anything you find that is top secret. Anything that will give us intel on our enemies."

Lena inclined her head. "Intel?"

He nodded. "Is that going to be a problem?"

Nausea climbed up Lena's throat. Things had gone far enough. "I will not do it. Irving is the furthest thing from a spy. He would never betray his country. Or his colleagues. He is proud to be an American. So are the others in the department. I will not stoop to your level."

"I'm glad you brought up the term 'American' Mrs. Stern,"

Collins said. "I have studied your background as well. I know you are a refugee from Germany. And a Jew."

There was just the slightest emphasis on the word "Jew."

"I am an American citizen. My husband worked at Met Lab. That is where we met."

"I am aware of that." He waved a hand. "But in this environment, in these times, one never knows who is a friend and who is an enemy. If you do not cooperate, your life—and that of your son could become—well . . . difficult."

"Are you threatening me, Colonel?" Lena said. She was shaking with rage now, not fear.

"Not at all, Mrs. Stern. Just reminding you of your duty as an American. Especially during a war in which enemies are all around us. Think it over."

CHAPTER 24

Lena couldn't sleep. She went to the kitchen, poured some of the whiskey she'd given Collins, and tossed it down. She had to tell Irving that Collins suspected him of espionage, but how could she do that without exposing herself? For all she knew, that was Collins's plan all along. He'd never liked her, and now he had a good reason to keep a close eye on her through Irving.

She was now going to be exploited by two groups, each for their own purposes. It didn't matter that Collins was clumsier and less sophisticated than the Germans. To both groups she was nothing more than a pawn, an insignificant player on a complicated chessboard. What would they do to her when she had served her purpose? What would they do to Max?

She covered her face with her hands. She was approaching a point of no return. Her days as a spy—perhaps even her days on this earth—were numbered. How had it come to this? Maybe she should have stayed in Germany with her family and Josef. She would undoubtedly be dead by now, but at least it would have been an honorable death. Unsullied by shame or scandal.

She paced back and forth in the living room. There might be someone whose help she could enlist. He'd been the one person—the only person—to suggest a connection between the groups. She had no reason to think he would help her; he might throw her to the wolves, like the others surely would. And if he did help, life would become more difficult. She tried to brainstorm other options, but she didn't see any.

She rummaged around the apartment for his card. He'd given it to her months earlier. She searched the kitchen, then the bedroom, but couldn't find it. She grew more frantic. She had to find it. She finally saw it in her jewelry box on the dresser. She grabbed it and practically ran to the telephone.

When he answered despite the late hour, she said breathlessly, "This is Lena Stern. You helped when my husband, Karl—was—died. And then when my son was kidnapped."

"Hello, Lena," Agent Lanier said. "I've been waiting for your call."

CHAPTER 25

The following morning ushered in a crisp fall day, the kind that evoked thoughts of a sweet New Year filled with apples and honey. The High Holidays had come and gone—they'd been early this year—but the swirl of scarlet, yellow, and orange leaves outside was a reminder of the season. Lena gave Max extra hugs before leaving for work.

She was under strict instructions not to tell Hans or Collins about her conversation with Lanier. He had come over after she called, and sat, ironically, in the same spot on the sofa as Collins. She'd told him everything. Then they'd discussed her options.

"I want you to work for us."

"Us?"

"The United States."

"I thought I already was. Through Collins."

"We haven't been able to pin him down. He may be a rogue agent, working for himself because he wasn't formally assigned to Manhattan. Or maybe he's something else. We just don't know."

"What do you want me to do?"

"Essentially, we want you to mix up your intel. Put misleading information in some of the documents you pass to Hans. Collins, too. Things that either mean nothing or are outright lies."

Lena bit her lip, thinking back to the sketch of the pile she'd altered. She told Lanier about it.

"Exactly. Good work. That's what we want."

"But how? How will I figure out what is meaningful and what isn't?"

"I'll let you know. I'll take a look at everything you're planning to pass. A day won't make much difference. You'll have to make sure I get a copy of everything before you send it on."

"How will I get it to you?"

"How do you do it now?"

She told him.

He nodded. "We'll set up our own dead drop."

She ran a hand through her hair. "What happens when they realize the documents have been adulterated?"

"They won't." He paused. "If you're careful. Remember, you're going to be passing them genuine intel also."

"To Collins, too, you say?"

Lanier nodded. "At this point, it's better to be safe than sorry, don't you agree?"

Lena didn't reply.

"Hey. I'm gonna do my best to back you up. You're working for the good guys now."

Skeptical, she flashed him a look. She'd worked for so many different people, she didn't trust anyone. How did she know Lanier was on the up-and-up? Shouldn't there be more serious repercussions? After all, she could be labeled a traitor by the FBI, and they would be right. Instead, they—or at least Lanier—wanted her to expand her duplicity. She raised a hand to her forehead. She wanted it all to end.

"Okay." Lanier shifted. She could smell his aftershave. "Now, let's talk about tomorrow."

• • •

Lena had two tasks. One, she was to tell Hans that Irving was now suspected of spying himself, and it was her fault. She would ask Hans what he could do to manage the situation. She would also talk about winding down her work. She would tell him she was prepared for the consequences, but she had to be honest; she was slowly going mad with guilt. Two, she would tell Irving about Collins's visit. He deserved to know he was under surveillance, she would say. Perhaps together they could come up with a solution to the colonel's scheming.

She wanted to talk to Irving right away, but she had to wait; he usually dropped by around lunchtime. Today, though, lunchtime came and went without him. Lena asked Sonia if she'd seen him. Sonia shook her head.

"But I have something to tell you."

Lena felt her stomach twist.

"I finally heard from Frank." Sonia grinned. "He's all right. He'll be coming home in a couple of months." Sonia's husband had been drafted and fought in the Battle of Midway over the summer, but Sonia hadn't heard from him in weeks.

A wave of relief so profound it came out as a gasp swept over Lena. "That's wonderful, Sonia. Congratulations!" She pasted on a smile and hoped it looked genuine.

"There's something else." Sonia tilted her head. "Once he's home, I—I won't be coming back."

"Oh no." Lena realized she had become fond of the girl. Not to mention that whoever replaced her might be a plant. She squeezed her eyes shut. She despised having to think this way.

"I am not as dedicated as you, Lena," Sonia added. "I could never spend all the time at work that you do." Dedicated? Was that what Sonia thought? Lena bit back a reply. She didn't want to spoil Sonia's joy.

• • •

Lena went to a pay phone after lunch and made a call.

"Where have you been, Irving? I've been so worried."

"I was fired."

"What? Why?"

"Collins knows I was in the pile when I wasn't supposed to be. The guard told him he heard two people. He didn't know the other, but he thought it was a woman. Collins thinks I'm a spy. He says he'll keep it under wraps if I go quietly."

"That's impossible. A spy? For whom?" Lena asked. She couldn't help wondering whether Collins knew the truth about *her*. Had he put the pieces together? Had his night visit been nothing but a ruse after all?

"For the Communists."

"The Communists? Wherever would he get that idea?" Inwardly, though, she let out a breath. She'd been handed a reprieve. Collins wasn't focusing on Nazi espionage. But her relief soon turned into self-loathing. How could she be thankful that the Nazis were off the hook?

"Irving?" There was no response. "Irving, we need to talk. This is all my fault."

Silence on his end. He wasn't disagreeing.

"Irving," she said, "I'm going to tell Collins I was the one who wanted to go in. If anything, I should be the one who's fired."

This time he answered. "No. There's no sense both of us suffering."

She'd hoped he'd say that. "But I can't let you take the blame when it was my idea." She pondered whether there really *was* any way to salvage the situation. Could she actually try to convince Collins that Irving was innocent? That it had been just an adventure? No. He'd never believe her. Either he'd think she was defending Irving, or he'd focus his suspicions on her. He probably had already. Then again, what did it matter? It was just a matter of time until she was exposed by Hans, Collins, perhaps even Lanier.

"No." Irving was firm. "You can't lose your job. I know how much you depend on it." He paused. "But I do have a question. Why did you want to see the pile so badly? Is there something I should know?"

Mein Gott. Lena stared at a sign for the dry cleaners across the street, but all she saw was a blurry mass of letters. She must not be a very good spy if her supposed boyfriend distrusted her. She wanted to melt into the ground, like that witch in the movie about Dorothy and the wizard. She answered carefully.

"Irving, you know me. What do you think?"

A long pause followed. Then: "I'm sorry, Lena. It's just this—all of this—is so alien to my whole being. My parents said I could move back in with them. But how can I? It—it would be admitting failure. If I can't work at Met Lab, I don't know what I'll do."

"You are not a spy, Irving. We both know it." She continued in a rush, grasping for something to say. "For all we know, Collins may be anti-Semitic. It wouldn't be surprising."

He sighed. "Anti-Jew, pro-Jew, who cares? It could be anyone . . . Sonia . . . you . . . me . . . even Compton, for Christ's sake. A cloud of suspicion can fall on anyone these days."

"Irving, stop!" What had she done to this wonderful young man? He was a shadow of what he had once been. A despondent, sad shadow. And it was her doing.

"Lena, I want to see you tonight. Please. Can I come over?"

She covered her eyes with one hand. She was meeting Hans that evening. She couldn't risk the two running into each other. She was just about to suggest the next night instead when he cut in.

"I understand." He'd mistaken the silence as her answer. "Good-bye, Lena."

"No, wait, Irving. That's not—"

But he'd hung up.

CHAPTER 26

Lena went through the next few hours like one of those zombies in a Bela Lugosi horror film. During the meeting with Hans in a coffee shop, she told him about Irving, how she'd been using him to get the sketch of the pile, and how it had backfired.

"You have to do something," she said, her voice full of anguish.

Hans shrugged.

"Please. I'm begging you."

"You are sure he doesn't know anything?"

She looked down, recalling Irving's question about whether there was anything he should know about her.

"What is it, Lena?" Hans sounded irritated.

She looked up. "He doesn't know anything. I'm sure of it."

"I see." Hans's eyes narrowed. She knew he didn't believe her.

• • •

Lena was surprised that no one at work talked about Irving. Or at least they didn't talk to her about him. She supposed people knew they'd been seeing each other and weren't sure what Lena's feelings were. In a way it was a blessing. She tried to concentrate on her work, but every time Collins came in, he'd stop to ask if she had any news, or make a comment that meant "Hurry up and get me something." She started to bite her nails, something she'd never done before. Headaches came and went. She lost her appetite and had trouble sleeping. Even Max couldn't chase away her bad moods.

A week later, toward the end of October, Lena came into work early, ostensibly to catch up on paperwork. She thought about photographing a letter or two but decided it was too risky. She never knew when Collins would show up.

It was a good decision; twenty minutes later Collins swept into the office. His usual bluster wasn't apparent; in fact, his facial muscles were stretched taut and his eyes radiated distress.

"Did you hear?"

Lena's pulse sped up. Collins rarely brought good news.

"There's been a terrible fire."

Lena jumped out of her chair, ran to a window, and looked out. No flames. No smell of smoke. "Where? I don't see anything." She turned around.

"Not here." He planted his hands on his hips. "Are you sure you haven't heard?"

"Colonel, I have no idea what you're talking about." Her heart pounded in her chest. "What—where is it?"

He paused for just a fraction of a second, then said, "Your beau. Irving Mandell. His parents' home burned down last night."

"Oh *mein Gott!*" Lena screamed. Her hands flew to the sides of her head.

"The fire department said a Halloween candle in the window somehow ignited the curtains beside it."

"But—but—," she sputtered. "That cannot be." Irving and his parents didn't celebrate Halloween. Irving had told Lena more than once that his family was observant. They would have considered Halloween a pagan ritual. Someone had deliberately set the fire and covered it up.

Collins went on. "Luckily, Mr. and Mrs. Mandell were not at home." He cleared his throat. "But Irving was."

Lena started to pull at her hair.

"He didn't make it, Mrs. Stern. He's gone."

•••

It didn't take long for the staff at Met Lab to start discussing the cause of the fire. Shock and horror quickly led to discussions about Irving, the abrupt end to his career, the rumors about espionage. Lena wasn't sure who first speculated that his death might not have been an accident. That Irving, morose and despondent at losing his job, had set it himself. Others pointed a finger at Collins and wanted him fired. They were sure Collins had somehow "arranged" the accident.

Lena knew better. Irving was distraught and depressed, but he would never have killed himself. And Collins didn't have the guts to make someone disappear. He was a bad man, a font of fear and suspicion, but he wasn't a killer.

She knew who had set the fire. And why. And with that knowledge, the last bit of her composure snapped. The situation was out of control. She had to protect Max. And herself. No matter what.

The following Saturday morning Lena told Mrs. M she had an

errand to run and asked Mrs. M to look after Max. She took the bus over to Chinatown, got off at Cermak and Wentworth, and headed south. At the corner of Twenty-Third Street, she turned right. Chen's Gun and Surplus occupied a shop in the middle of the block. Lena pushed through the door. Thirty minutes later she left with a Smith and Wesson .22 revolver and a box of bullets.

CHAPTER 27

Chicago, November 1942

Lena didn't know how she got through the month of November. Spying for both Hans and Collins, and reporting to Lanier as well, was nearly an impossible balancing act. And it was a performance—for Hans, for Collins, even for Lanier. She felt like an actor playing three roles, and she had to keep track of what she said to whom. If she dropped just one line to the wrong player, she would be exposed, even possibly killed, faster than Superman's speeding bullet.

At least with Hans, she didn't have to worry about a physical copy of the intelligence she passed, genuine or not; the film from the Minox was a lifesaver. But Collins and Lanier required actual documents. She normally used carbon paper for the copies she typed, so she added two more sheets, but when the copies weren't perfectly aligned, they jammed in the roller and looked messy. Occasionally Lena would glance over at Sonia, afraid that that the woman would see what she was doing, but Sonia was preoccupied with her husband's return and seemed oblivious.

Incoming letters and memos had to be copied by hand. She started to sneak documents into her bag to take home to copy once Max was asleep. She was careful to disguise her penmanship, in the event someone from the department might try to link it to her. Of course, it was easier to alter the documents that way. But there was also the problem of passing the materials. Collins maintained he had a top security clearance. But when she asked Lanier, he'd told her the man was lying. Still, she had no choice. She had to deliver the intel.

The first piece she passed Collins was a letter from Compton to the army with an analysis of the latest news from Berkeley, California. J. Robert Oppenheimer was supervising the work of a group of theoretical physicists that included Felix Bloch, Hans Bethe, Edward Teller, Robert Serber, and John H. Manley from Chicago's Met Lab. The group decided they would need twice as much fissionable material as they'd previously estimated to build the bomb. In the letter Compton had reserved judgment until the pile yielded results.

At lunchtime Lena folded the letter, threw on her coat and gloves, and told Sonia she was going for a walk. Before going downstairs, she stopped in the ladies' room and slipped the copy of the letter inside one of her gloves. Outside, she bumped into Collins as they'd planned and casually dropped the glove on the ground. Collins bent over and picked it up.

That afternoon, he showed up in the office. "Ladies." He waved a red glove in Sonia and Lena's direction. "Do you have any idea who this belongs to? I found it outside."

Sonia looked over at Lena. "Isn't that part of the pair you just bought, Lena?"

Lena looked up in surprise. "Why, yes. It is. Thank you, Colonel. I must have dropped it when I went to lunch."

• • •

That night Lena stayed late to finish her work. She had just put on her coat to leave when Collins appeared at the door. She hated how he seemed to slip in and out of the shadows.

He flashed her a suspicious look. "How did you know I want intel on Oppenheimer?"

She shook her head. "I didn't."

His eyebrows arched.

"Colonel, I assume you want any information on the Manhattan Project that seems relevant. And to which you are not otherwise privy," she couldn't help adding.

He stiffened. "Well, then." He cleared his throat. "Fate has intervened. I want whatever you can find on Oppenheimer. What he thinks, what he does, how much money he has, what he spends it on. When he takes a shower or cheats on his wife. Anything and everything."

Lena didn't reply.

"You know who he is," Collins went on.

"He's a colleague of Professor Compton's and a brilliant physicist."

"He is also known to associate with Communists, and we have a strong suspicion he is one himself. In fact, he is the reason I'm here. This man may well become the leader of the Manhattan Project when construction begins. We must keep a close eye on him." He paused. "Good work."

Lena walked home slowly. She couldn't do it anymore. This was insanity. She would certainly be exposed, and the retribution, from the Nazis or Collins or even Lanier, would ruin her. It had to end, one way or another, despite what the three men wanted. Fortunately, she had an idea how to stir things up, perhaps push events toward a speedy conclusion. When she got home she signaled for a meeting with Hans.

CHAPTER 28

"There's been a complication," she told Hans when they met the next day.

"What?" Hans asked.

She told him about Collins. "I wanted to tell you before, but I have been afraid. I do not know how much he knows about my—our—situation. I wanted to be sure before I came to you."

Hans's face was unreadable. "What have you been passing to him?"

"Pretty much the same thing I've given you."

Hans grunted. "Make sure you tell me exactly what material he gets from now on." He appraised her. "Does he have any idea about our arrangement?"

"That's why I waited. He does not know. I am sure."

She expected Hans to be suspicious, to threaten reprisals, to punish her in some way. To her surprise, though, he smiled. "Well, well, this could actually be quite useful. Make sure you continue to update me on him."

Update him? That was all? Lena tensed. Hans really did seem unconcerned. But they'd had Irving killed for getting in the way. Her plan wasn't working. "How can you say Collins *might* be useful? He's a serious threat."

"What makes you believe that?"

Lena felt her anger build. "Hans, look at the situation. You have me spying for the Germans. Collins has me spying on the Communists. If he finds out, I am finished. Especially now that Hitler has invaded Russia."

"Lena, do not worry."

He was trying to soothe her. Badly, she thought. "You seem to forget it is my life at stake."

"You are doing a wonderful job."

She took a deep breath. "No. This cannot continue. I want out. That's why I told you about Collins. It has become too dangerous. I cannot do this anymore. *Genug ist genug.*"

Hans nodded. "I understand. It will not be long now."

"What do you mean?"

"We all know that when construction begins, the Manhattan Project will relocate to other places. You will, of course, remain here. The only question is when the move will take place. We will reassess your options at that point."

"But what about Collins? What are you going to do about him?"

Hans seemed unperturbed. "Nothing. He's—what do the Americans say? 'Small potatoes.'"

Lena knew she would go straight to hell for thinking it, but she couldn't wait for the bomb to be built. At least she would be free.

If she was still alive.

CHAPTER 29

Chicago, December 1942

The moment everyone at Met Lab had been working toward happened at three thirty p.m. on Wednesday, December 2. One of Fermi's assistants moved the last control rod into place, and at three twenty-five, the core began to feed on itself. At three thirty, Chicago Pile Number One, the mountain of graphite, uranium metal, and uranium oxide, produced the first self-sustaining nuclear chain reaction. The power level was only half a watt, but nobody cared. The reactor worked!

Compton immediately called James Conant, the National Defense Research Committee chairman, and, speaking in code, said, "The Italian navigator has just landed in the New World."

"Were the natives friendly?" Conant asked.

"Everyone landed safe and happy."

• • •

The celebration at a nearby bar was long-lived and raucous, if a group of physicists could be called raucous. No one was happier than Lena. The next phase of the bomb's development would begin, but her work would end. She couldn't wait. She was going to quit her job and find something completely different: a position at an insurance company or a manufacturing plant. She'd had enough of science she didn't understand, as well as the duplicity she understood too well. The money would be a loss, but the chance to regain her self-respect would more than make up for it.

Over the next few days, Met Lab scientists raised the power inside the pile to two hundred watts to make sure the chain reaction hadn't been a fluke. That afternoon one of the scientists came out of the pile with burns on his arms. Lena didn't say anything, but she knew that radiation, a by-product of the chain reaction, was dangerous. Three days later, that scientist became ill; by the end of the week he was dead. It was a devastating blow. In a way Lena was glad Irving was no longer with them. He would have died for the Manhattan Project, too. In fact, he had.

CHAPTER 30

A few days later, Lena was filing a top secret memo to Compton from Groves. In her impatience to photograph it, she almost missed it, but the word "Germany" drew her attention. Groves reported something they'd suspected and now had confirmed. The Germans had given up serious atomic research at least a year earlier. Possibly more. Hitler simply did not have the resources or manpower to experiment. Finances were a huge drain now that the Nazis were fighting a two-front war. Every available *Reichsmark* had been allocated to the Wehrmacht.

Lena's eyes widened. For the past six months, she, like everyone else at Met Lab, believed Nazi Germany was an existential threat to America. That German scientists were working furiously on atomic weapons development, and, in fact, were ahead of the US. Now it appeared the opposite was the truth. What she and everyone else had been told was just propaganda. Lies. A way, perhaps, to get the Americans to work longer, harder, faster.

She finished photographing the memo with her Minox and

slipped the film into the dead drop on the way home. She knew it would trigger a reaction. She was ostensibly spying for the Germans. The same Germans who were *not* working on an atom bomb. So if the Germans weren't making a bomb, why was she spying for them? True, they might want information anyway, but why the urgency? The cloak-and-dagger meetings and signals? Moreover, if the Germans were designating every mark for the Wehrmacht, where did the money she'd been given come from?

She thought back over the events of the past year, starting with Karl's death last December. A death that had never been resolved. Then Max's kidnapping in April, which had not been solved either. Irving had died in a mysterious fire that October, after she'd made him show her the pile. Three tragic events in twelve months. They weren't all coincidence. She'd known that, deep within her subconscious, but she hadn't wanted to admit it.

But now she had to. Her survival depended on it. Hans and his Nazi companions had orchestrated everything. Killing Karl was the first step. It had made her penniless and vulnerable. Then they'd abducted Max, returning him only when she agreed to work for them. Finally, they'd gotten rid of Irving—he was a complication they didn't need.

And now they would be closing in on her. When they figured out she knew it had all been a ruse, what would they do? She recalled how vague Hans had been about her future once the Manhattan Project moved. What if she had no future? What if she was nothing more than a pawn in their operation? Unimportant. Expendable.

A wave of hot emotion rolled over her. She explored it. Tasted it. For once it wasn't fear. It was anger. An anger approaching fury.

After everything that had been done to her and her loved ones, how could she let them make her superfluous?

When she got home, she fixed dinner, then played Lincoln Logs with Max until bedtime. Once he was asleep, she tried to come up with a plan. She could go to Collins and confess she was a double agent. Expose Hans and his people. But Collins had never trusted her, despite the fact that she was passing him intelligence. He would accuse her of treason, and he'd be right. He wouldn't understand the desperation of a mother forced to protect her child. She would certainly spend the rest of her life in prison. She might even be executed.

She slumped on the sofa, head in her hands. Lanier was no guarantee of safe passage either. He hadn't made any promises. He'd simply said that, in return for her compliance, he would try to "back her up." She was truly *gefickt*.

She went to the closet and retrieved the .22. She brought it back to the living room and raised it in the air. Then she aimed it an imaginary target. Could she do it for real? Her throat closed up. She wasn't sure. All she knew was that they would not—could not—win. Not this time. She knew something else, too. Her days as a spy were at an end. No more deception. No more duplicity.

She picked up the phone.

CHAPTER 31

The next day Lena spotted the signal from Hans on her way back from lunch with Sonia. A miniature American flag stood in a snow-covered urn in front of the Fifty-Seventh Street florist. He wanted to meet her after work. She considered not showing up. But if she didn't, Hans would come after her or, worse, Max. So when she got home, she went to the closet, loaded the .22, and slipped it into her coat pocket. At least she would have the element of surprise.

The Ford rolled up a few minutes later. On this typical winter day in Chicago, the sun was setting, but it had snowed a few inches the night before, and the bite in the air required gloves, hats, and scarves. Lena waited until the car stopped and the window rolled down.

Hans called out from the driver's seat. "Come in and get warm."

Only after she slid into the passenger seat did she realize another man was in back. She turned around to take a look. He was a beefy, muscled bull of a man. That chilled her more than the frigid December weather.

"Who is this?" she asked.

Hans waved a hand. "This is Dieter."

The man looked up at the mention of his name.

"He doesn't speak English," Hans said.

"Why is he here?"

"I'm training him," Hans said, but the pause before he spoke told her that was a lie.

Lena's thoughts darkened. Dieter had to be an assassin, and she was his target. He was there to "deal" with her. She bit her lip. She briefly thought of escaping. Throwing herself out of the car. The Ford was heading south on Lake Shore Drive. But timing was everything. She'd have to scoot to the edge of the seat, fling open the car door, and propel herself onto the road. And she'd have to make sure other traffic was far enough behind that she wouldn't be run over. She let out a frustrated breath. There were too many variables. She couldn't do it.

She hoped Hans would turn in at one of the beaches along the drive. Maybe then she could make her move. Sure enough, at Seventy-Seventh Street, Hans turned into Rainbow Beach and Park, a peninsula that jutted out onto the lake. A wide expanse of lawn with picnic tables and a sandy beach beyond, it was always crowded in summer. She and Karl had come here to admire the view of the Loop to the north, which on sunny summer days was so spectacular it should have been on one of those picture postcards. Now, though, with its skeletal tree branches, and grass that was brown and brittle and covered with snow, the park was as empty and desolate as an abandoned graveyard.

"Why are we here?" Lena asked.

"We wanted a place where we wouldn't be interrupted. You have been asking questions. It's time to give you some answers."

She stole a glance at Hans. What game was he playing? The only answer she expected was a loaded pistol aimed at her. Hans pulled around a graceful drive that led to a squat building bordering the lake and parked. He switched off the ignition and motioned for her to open the door.

"Now we walk."

They got out of the car and started across the park away from the lake. Hans and Dieter flanked her. Dusk plunged the park into shadow, which softened the definition of objects, making them difficult to identify. She slipped her hands in her pockets, felt the comforting weight of her revolver. At least she wasn't without some defense.

Beyond a stand of trees was a picnic table covered with a layer of snow. As they approached, a figure emerged from the gloom—a man wrapped up in what looked like a black Chesterfield coat, a black fedora on his head, sturdy boots on his feet. Something was familiar about him. The shape of his head. The sharp edge of his chin. The lift of his shoulders. Lena's heart banged in her chest. She knew this man. She quickened her pace.

He studied her as she approached, his body angled toward hers in a way she remembered well. As she closed in, he gave her a smile.

Lena sucked in a breath. "Josef!"

CHAPTER 32

Josef's smile widened. "Hello, Lena."

Lena had forgotten her boots, and enough snow had seeped into her shoes to make her shiver. But the block of ice in her heart made her feet feel hot. "I—I do not understand. What are you doing here?"

He extended his hands, which were encased in thick leather gloves. "I am here for you."

"For me?" Lena blinked in a daze of confusion. "What do you mean? How long have you been in America?"

"Long enough."

"Why did you not contact me?"

He paused. "I did. Through Hans. I have known every move you've made."

"But you were in Budapest. How did you—"

A trace of irritation unfolded across his face. "You never used to be this slow, Lena. Hans mentioned how tentative you have become. Now I see he was right."

Lena scowled.

He paused and took a breath. When he spoke again his tone was conciliatory. "I'm sorry. I know how much you've been through. It would make anyone uncertain."

Lena took a good look at him. Josef seemed older; she thought she spotted a touch of gray at his temples. But he was still tall. And strong. With the Aryan look that had always made her feel part proud, part ashamed. He was watching her with an expectant expression, and she realized she was supposed to say something.

"How—how did you find me? We haven't been in touch."

"Oh, Lena." He spread his hands. "Think. It is quite simple."

She squinted in concentration. When it came to her, she took a few steps back, and her mouth dropped open. "You! You've been directing the operation."

He dipped his head in acknowledgment.

"But—but . . . ," she sputtered. "How? Why? You are a Jew."

He shrugged.

A streak of fury shot up her spine. "You passed, didn't you?" she hissed. She recalled how they had joked years ago that with his blond hair and green eyes, he could.

He turned up his palms. "I didn't need to." He ran a gloved hand along the edge of the picnic table and scooped up a mound of snow. He shaped it into a ball. "Hans has been my eyes and ears."

She spun around. Hans stood behind her. His chin jutted out as if he was trying not to be embarrassed.

"We had to wait for the right moment to tell you." Josef smiled again.

"Tell me what, Josef?"

He turned away, tossed the snowball across the park, turned back. "Shortly after I arrived in Budapest, my parents and I were starving. We didn't have work; we didn't have money. One day I was approached by two men near the synagogue. They bought me a few meals. I was grateful. It was the first time my belly was full since . . . Well. We started to talk. We all agreed that the Nazis had to be defeated. They remarked that I could pass. With my looks . . . Well, you know."

She tightened her lips.

"And, well, eventually the enemy of my enemy became my friend. Not so very different than you and your Colonel Collins."

A fresh wave of anger took Lena's breath away. "Communists!" She gasped. "You are working for the Communists! All this time I have been spying for them, not the Nazis." She slipped her hands back in her pockets and felt for the gun.

Josef didn't deny it. "At first I did low-level operations in and around Budapest. But when you wrote that you were working in the Physics Department at the University of Chicago . . . well, everyone became very excited."

Lena squeezed her eyes shut. She had mentioned her job in a letter. More than once. She remembered describing everyone in the department to him. In retrospect, how could she have been so naïve? She knew the answer. She had been in love. She had wanted to share everything with this man.

"In fact, you were responsible for my rise in the ranks, Lena. Moscow is quite specific about the intelligence they want from their American cells. They want updates on the Met Lab project. The procedures being used for U-235 separation. The method of detonation that will be used. What industrial equipment is used to test these techniques. You have access to all of it."

The anger roiling her gut curled it into a tight ball. Blood drained from her head.

"So, you see, it could not have been more perfect. You fell into my hands." He looked pleased with himself. "The rest was easy."

"Easy? You lied to me. You told me I was spying for the Nazis. You forced me to go back to work after Karl—" She cut herself off. "You! You were the one who killed my husband."

He looked down. It was the first time she thought he might have felt a shred of regret. "Let's just say I let it happen. "

"You excuse murder by claiming you 'let it happen'? What kind of man have you become, Josef? Why did you not ask me? Perhaps I would have..." Her voice trailed off when she noticed Josef rummage in his coat pocket. She gripped the revolver. But when his hand emerged, it was clutching a pack of cigarettes. He pulled one out, lit it with a match, and exhaled a cloud of smoke. When had he picked up that habit?

"Come, Lena. Do not be naïve. You would never have worked for us willingly."

"But why did you lie about the Nazis? Do you know what guilt—what self-loathing it caused me?"

"We had to protect ourselves. We had no idea you would turn out to be such a valuable asset. If you had been caught, we wanted your superiors to think the Germans were behind it, not us."

"So you tore apart my soul and ruined my life... for your protection."

He stiffened. "As you did mine. You left me for another man." For a moment his composure slipped and his features hardened. This was no longer the Josef she knew.

"For which you took revenge by killing him." She paused. The pieces were coming together now. "And then you kidnapped Max."

Josef's demeanor changed again, and he resumed his civilized manner. "He is quite the young boy. I entertained him myself. Such a bright, curious child. I wish he was my son."

Lena ignored that. "And then there was Irving."

Josef blew out smoke. She inhaled the odor of stale tobacco. "He was in your way. He would have been trouble. He became what they call collateral damage."

"Collateral damage," she whispered.

He flicked the cigarette into the snow. She watched the orange tip flicker out.

"I am sorry for your pain. I was just following orders."

She tried to keep the shrillness out of her voice. "And are you following them now?"

He glanced at Hans and Dieter. "Now I make them. That is why I am here. I want to make amends. I know you are boxed in with Collins. It has become dangerous. You cannot go back to work. I want to offer you a way out. Come with me." He hesitated. "We will go to New York and disappear. I will be a father to Max."

She flinched. "But you are married. To the girl you told me about."

He smiled. "A white lie. There is no other. There has never been anyone but you, Lena. I did this for us." He waved a hand. "Come home to me. Hashem has a way of balancing the scales. We can wipe away the past. Give ourselves a clean slate."

Lena recoiled at his chutzpah. No, not just chutzpah. Arrogance. Unmitigated arrogance. Was it really this easy for him to come full circle?

Josef smiled, almost as if he knew what she was thinking.

She covered her mouth with her hand. Maybe she had no other choice. He was right. She couldn't go back to Met Lab. Which meant she would have no way to support herself and Max. But if she went back to Josef, how could she survive? This man might have been her first love, but what she saw in him now frightened and disgusted her. How could he expect the past seven years to evaporate, to disappear into the fog of the past as easily as shadows grow into night? She would live in a constant state of fear, perhaps even terror. No. It was wrong. Everything was wrong.

"You used me. Manipulated me. Killed my husband. Kidnapped my son. Drove me to the edge of insanity."

"I will make it up to you. I promise." He ran his hand along the table and scooped up more snow.

She tried to suppress her revulsion. All the misery, the sorrow and guilt, was carved into the marrow of her bones. He couldn't wipe it away with a scoop of clean snow and sweet words. She wrapped her fingers around the Smith and Wesson in her pocket. "Because you want to balance the scales."

He nodded. "We are meant to be together. Ever since we promised each other in the Tiergarten. Until death do us part. Do you remember?"

She drew two steps closer. "I do. And I believe you are right. It is time to balance the scales."

He opened his arms.

"Until death do us part," she said.

Before she could change her mind, she pulled out the gun and fired. As Josef crumpled to the ground, she spun around and shot Hans. He fell backward. She whirled around. She knew shooting two and not the third was as bad as shooting none. And Dieter was coming at her, his gun aimed at her chest. She dropped to the ground, hoping to make herself a smaller target. But it was too late. Two more shots rang out.

CHAPTER 33

Lena watched as Dieter slowly collapsed a few yards away, his blood staining the snow red. She rolled on the snow and pulled herself to a sitting position. Dazed, she touched her chest, her arms, her face. Her ears rang with the reverberation of the shots, but she was alive. And she wasn't wounded. Dieter was dead.

Gradually her ears cleared, and she heard the wail of sirens. About a dozen men swarmed across the field, most of them shouting. She watched in a detached, confused state, unsure what was happening. Then, through the blur of motion, she heard a familiar voice. "Lena, are you all right? Answer me."

She tried to focus.

Agent Lanier appeared in her sight line. He ran over, crouched down, and draped his arm around her shoulder. "You're okay. Do you understand? Its over."

"I—I shot them," she whispered.

"Yes. You did."

Lanier glanced over at Josef and Hans. Lena followed his gaze.

Hans lay unmoving, but Josef was writhing on the ground, moaning. Lanier's men surrounded him, blocking her view.

"Dieter was going to shoot me. How . . .?" She looked up at him.

"We got him first."

She blinked several times, trying to process the information. "But how did you know we were here?"

"We've been tailing you all day. Ever since you called last night. I haven't been more than a few feet away."

She licked her lips. The frigid air made them sting. "I had to do it. After what he did . . . to me . . . and Karl . . . and . . ."

Lanier cut her off. "Lena . . . do you realize what you've done?"

"I committed murder. Twice."

Lanier shook his head. "You have broken up one of the most important Communist espionage rings in the United States."

Her brow furrowed. "No. You don't understand. I—I . . ."

"Shhh." He raised a finger to his lips. "I know you're upset. You're probably in shock. But you are a hero, Lena. No one has ever done what you have. For as long as you." He took a breath. "You have been privy to the inner workings of a major spy ring. And Josef, the leader of the cell, is still alive."

Four men bent down, lifted Josef off the ground, and carried him to a waiting ambulance.

They both watched in silence. For Lena it was surreal. Then she asked, "What happens now?"

Lanier smiled. "We'll make sure his wounds heal. Then turn him, of course."

"Turn him?"

"Don't worry. You won't be involved. You've already told me everything you passed him."

"But wait." She raised her palms in a warding-off gesture. "What about Colonel Collins? What is he going to do?"

"He's been informed. He's elated. He's calling you a true patriot."

"But I committed treason."

Lanier leaned over and offered his hand to help her up. "You were forced to. Fortunately, you came to me in time. You've been a double . . . no . . . a triple agent during a time of war for your country."

She frowned. "Are you saying you knew Hans and Josef weren't Nazis? Did you know they were Communists?"

He didn't answer for a moment. Then he hung his head. "I told you before. I've been working on this case for over a year, Lena."

"So that means yes?"

He nodded.

She dropped her hand from his. Her expression turned steely. "Why didn't you tell me?"

A pleading look came over him. "I wanted to. My superiors forbade it. They were afraid you wouldn't work as hard against the Communists as you would against the Nazis. After all, Nazis are your mortal enemies."

She gazed at him. In a way, he was no different from Hans or Collins. He'd been manipulating her too. Using her. She should hate him. Except that he had just saved her life.

"Not telling you was wrong," Lanier went on. "We know that now. You've proven that you are willing to sacrifice your life for America. You are a star, Lena. In fact, there are a lot of people who want to shake your hand."

She stood up unsteadily. Her world had suddenly turned upside down.

"But I'll bet you just want to go home to your son."

She nodded.

"Look. I have work to do, but I'll come by as soon as I can. We have a lot to talk about." He called out to one of the men. "Archer, take the lady home, will you?" He turned back to her. "People will be talking about you for years to come, Lena."

She shook her head in confusion. "You're talking as if I am someone special. But I'm not."

He laughed. "Oh, but you're wrong. *I'm* nothing special. A normal red-blooded American. Born and bred in Iowa. *You* are remarkable."

"Normal," she repeated. Perhaps he was right. She'd been a refugee, a widow, a spy, and now, apparently, a patriot. Since she'd come to America, she'd never been normal. Even though that was the only thing she'd ever wanted.

"Normal," she said. "An average American. What does that feel like?"

"Maybe it's time you learned." He took her elbow and guided her across the field to the car. "We can talk about that, too."

"Yes. Let's." She smiled.

P.O.W.

CHAPTER 1

Mary-Catherine

I was milking the cows when the prisoners arrived. It was just after sunrise on a bright September morning, and I was still sleepy. Mama used to brew coffee every morning, and its rich aroma was my signal to roll out of bed, dress, and steal a few minutes with her before we set to our chores. But coffee had been rationed three months earlier, and the scent of morning was gone. Mama did manage to snag some Postum in town, but it wasn't the same, and I'd begun sleeping through dawn. Now Mama had to yell up the stairs, "Mary-Catherine, get your heinie out of bed."

Our postdawn talks had changed too, although the lack of coffee had nothing to do with that. I'd turned eighteen six months earlier, and Mama started treating me more like an adult. It was about time. Sometimes she'd tell me all the gossip she picked up in town, and we'd giggle or sympathize depending on whether we liked the people involved. Mostly, though, she'd share her fears about the war, the crops, and Dad coming home safely.

The war had stolen the last traces of my childhood. I was a woman now, but for three years, since I was fifteen, I'd spent most of my time away from school laboring on the farm. Before the war, Mama milked the cows and I fed the chickens. But when Dad was drafted, we all moved up a notch. Mama drove the tractor, and I milked the cows. My nine-year-old brother, Harley, fed the chickens, my old job. Seven-year-old Leanne fed the cats.

That morning I trudged off to the barn to milk Gretel and Rosie. I'd started on Gretel when I heard a loud honk and the screech of brakes in need of a lube job. Rosie could wait. I hurried out of the barn.

Reinhard

We jounced along a country road somewhere north of Chicago: ten of us shackled together with leg irons. The others didn't appear to mind, but I was humiliated. Of course, that was precisely what the Americans wanted.

I still found it difficult to believe we had been captured. One day we were the Twenty-First Panzer Division fighting with Field Marshal Rommel in Tunisia; the next we were chained like dogs. The blasted Italians and French! Damn them to hell. The Italians strutted around like fat chickens. And the French had proven to be—well—French. Sniffing out the situation, then weaseling their way into the most advantageous position. They proved their duplicity when their damnable Vichy troops switched sides to fight with the Free French forces. The Führer rightly retaliated and expanded our occupation to the whole of France, not just the North.

The truck slowed. We made a sharp turn and bumped down a

dirt path studded with stones. On one side was an apple orchard; on the other, I learned later, a field of soybeans. It was early fall and we were to help with the harvest for a week or two.

At the end of the path, in front of a small white clapboard farmhouse with sagging eaves, stood a family. No husband or father. He was no doubt in the military, perhaps already dead. The farmwife stood with arms crossed, a haggard and worried frown on her face. Behind her was a young woman peeking over her shoulder with a curious gaze, like we were the circus coming to town. Clinging to their mother's apron strings, two wide-eyed children stared as if we were evil trolls from one of the Grimms' fairy tales.

Wilhelm

The sun crested the horizon, glinting over green and tawny fields as we approached the farm. The guards had chained us together for the journey but promised to remove the restraints when we reached our destination. Most of the men were used to the practice. Still, one or two grimaced with angry lips.

I didn't know the men with me. I hadn't fought with them and had no particular allegiance to them. I missed my comrades. There were seven of us at the beginning of Operation Capri, but at the end of the Battle of Medenine we were only three, and they split us up when they sent us to America.

The voyage across the ocean was a disaster. Although the meals prepared for us were ample and tasted better than the meager portions we were allotted in the Wehrmacht, I was prone to seasickness and lost so much weight that the ship doctor was concerned.

After we landed, we were processed and delegated to trains that carried us to various destinations across America. I was sent to Camp Skokie Valley, not far from Chicago, with nearly two hundred other POWs. Most of us were assigned to nearby orchards and farms. A few lucky ones would work at the Naval Air Station. I had hoped to be assigned there; I'd always wanted to be a pilot, and liked being around planes, but I had the unfortunate circumstance of wearing glasses and wasn't accepted.

The truck made a sharp turn, and we headed down a dirt road. I gazed at the waves of grain. That phrase was in one of the American anthems, I recalled. The stalks of wheat and sorghum I'd seen on the train from Newport News to Chicago swayed back and forth in the breeze. The songwriter must have been a poet.

Then I caught sight of the family at whose farm we would be working. A woman, two little children at her side. And a second woman, younger, not much older than a girl. As we drew closer, I could see she was quite attractive: long chestnut hair, blue eyes with thick lashes, and a trim figure. The children seemed to be afraid; then again, who could blame them? The mother seemed apprehensive. I wondered what the young woman was thinking. I studied her more closely. She quite took my breath away. She was not simply attractive; she was beautiful.

CHAPTER 2

Mary-Catherine

I watched the men in the truck. Mama was beside me, fidgeting with her apron. The truck driver and another soldier climbed out of the cab. Both in uniform, the driver was short and pudgy, the passenger tall and skinny. They reminded me of Mutt and Jeff in the Sunday comics. I nervously pulled up my bobby sox, which I wore with my farm boots.

The tall skinny man smiled as he approached. Mama stepped forward. She had to crane her neck up to talk to him. They spoke quietly, and I couldn't make out the conversation, but she nodded several times. At one point, the soldier's eyebrows arched, and he seemed pleased. He led Mama to the truck. The chubby soldier unshackled the prisoners. Several massaged their ankles, but no one made a move to get down.

"Prisoners, there is good news," the tall man said.

Then Mama did something I'd never heard her do. She spoke to them in German!

"*Guten tag. Herzlich Willkommen auf unserer Farm und Zuhause.*"
She paused. "I hope we can work together in harmony."

My mouth dropped open. I'd heard Mama use a word or two of German, but I didn't know she knew the language so well. Where had she learned?

The prisoners seemed to be pleased to have been welcomed in their mother tongue. They jostled each other, exchanged glances, and grinned. Except for one. He remained stone-faced, arms crossed, eyes narrowed. What he was thinking?

"*Ich kenne nur ein wenig Deutsch,*" Mama went on. "But between us, we will understand each other, yes?"

The men replied in a chorus of "Yah's" and even an "Okay" or two.

"What'd you just say, Mama?" I asked when she came back over.

She whispered, "I told them that I only know a little German."

"Okay. You heard the lady." The stocky driver made a sweeping gesture with his arm. "Everybody out. Mrs. O'Rourke will tell you where to go and what to do."

I edged toward her. "Where did you learn to speak German so well, Mama? How did you—"

She shushed me. "I'll tell you later, sweetheart."

Ten prisoners emerged from the bed of the truck. The tall skinny guard picked up a rifle and held it close by his side. The men eyed me. I eyed them right back. None looked much older than me. They wore short-sleeved denim shirts open at the top, white undershirts poking out. Their solid white baggy pants were stitched or inked with the letters "P-O-W." They were orderly and polite. Even Harley let go of Mama's apron strings to peer at the men through his thick glasses.

When Harley was a baby, he had been struck with scarlet fever and it had affected his vision. He was the only student in his class to wear glasses, and the other kids made fun of him. He'd become pretty sensitive about it.

I pointed to one of the prisoners, who was also wearing specs. "Look, Harley, that prisoner wears glasses, too!"

Harley almost smiled. And then my gaze moved to the man standing directly behind him. Mr. Stone Face. There was something about him. I couldn't look away. Was it his straw-colored blond hair? His eyes? His skin, already tanned from the summer sun? Was he angry about being shipped to a boring farm like ours? I could relate. I sometimes felt like a prisoner myself.

Even though he was stone-faced, he seemed to know who he was and where he was going. Maybe it was the way he carried himself. He reminded me of my high school boyfriend, Steve. He'd get something in his mind, some cockamamie plan, and nothing could stop him. He was determined to enlist in the air force. Not the army. Not the navy. He wanted to fly bombers. He got his wish, too. Until his plane was shot down over the Pacific.

The German soldier looked at me. For just a second, our eyes met. Did he smile at me? The corner of his mouth turned up a bit; I think it was a smile. Then he lifted his arm and gave me a tiny wave. I felt giddy.

Reinhard

I shuddered when the woman spoke to us in German. Hers was the most atrocious accent I'd ever heard. A child could have done better. These Americans. They think they can do anything. They claim the moral high ground and believe they are beyond criticism. But their pride destroys civilizations, like this woman destroys our mother tongue.

"Work together in harmony"? Was that a joke? We were to be paid for our trouble. Five dollars a day. A pittance, at best. I nudged Franz and rolled my eyes. Of all the soldiers I'd met since arriving at camp, Franz was the only person I might call a friend. Like me, he'd been on the officer track in the SS before we were conscripted. Now, though, Franz did not acknowledge my gesture. He seemed interested in the family. Surely he wouldn't be taken in by these peasants?

The family was pathetic. Their clothes were as shabby as their home. They would be ostracized in Deutschland for allowing their home to deteriorate to such a point. A young boy wearing spectacles sidled over to the young woman, attractive for an Irish mongrel. She smiled, put an arm around him, and pointed to Stemm, who wore glasses as well. I couldn't remember Stemm's Christian name. Wilhelm, perhaps?

The boy grinned at Stemm. Stemm smiled back, for a moment, but I realized he was smiling at the young woman, not the boy. To be honest, she wasn't bad looking. German blood must run through her.

It was then, at precisely that moment, that an idea occurred to me. When it was my turn to climb down from the truck, I got the woman's attention and waved. She waved back, then looked ashamed to have done so. I was happy to see that Stemm witnessed the entire exchange.

Wilhelm

It doesn't matter how large or small a group is; there is bound to be someone who is disgruntled. Germany was being outspent, outgunned, and outmaneuvered by the Allies. But Reinhard Deschler refused to believe it. Arrogant and judgmental, he stomped around the camp, complaining bitterly about the war, the barracks, the food, even his fellow prisoners.

Most of the German POWs in America were Wehrmacht, the German armed forces. But there were also SS and Nazis, and a handful of Abwehr, German military intelligence. For the most part, the Wehrmacht soldiers understood that we had fought nobly, but we had been overpowered. Although we were disappointed and even resentful at first, once we settled down we recognized that for us, the war was over. We wished only for a speedy end to the hostilities.

Among the ranks of Nazis and SS, however, there were some who clung to the illusion that the Reich and Hitler would prevail. Their smug Nazi superiority surfaced far too often. Deschler was one of the zealots. Either he and the others like him were in complete denial, or—and I had considered this—the war had driven them mad.

To be fair, the Americans had treated us well. We were permitted to buy clothing, books, and writing utensils. Even beer. In the evenings, we watched movies or played cards. Occasionally the guards brought us ice cream or pastries. In fact, some of the men whispered that they did not wish to return to Germany, although the Geneva Conventions required it. We showered daily and roamed freely within the camp—although with the barbed wire, we did not go far. Still, it was sometimes possible to imagine we weren't prisoners at all but simple laborers. The guards claimed they treated us the way they hoped their own POWs would be treated by the Nazis.

Small chance of that.

And yet, Deschler and, to a lesser extent, his lapdog, Franz Wendt, seemed offended by the treatment. I tried to give Deschler a wide berth, but it was my bad luck to be assigned to the same work detail.

Now, as we approached the farm, I watched as Reinhard sprang down from the truck, lithe and graceful, like a tiger on the prowl. When he did, he waved and threw a dazzling smile to the girl I thought so attractive. She returned the wave; indeed, she could hardly tear her eyes away. At the conclusion of his little act, he looked back at me with a sneer. He wanted to make sure I'd seen it.

I rubbed the back of my neck, already damp with sweat. The guards had told me that summers on the prairie could be blistering hot. They were right.

CHAPTER 3

Mary-Catherine

"Where did you learn to speak German so well?" I asked Mama that evening as we prepared supper.

She peeled the last of five potatoes and slid them into the pot. Before she could answer, Leanne burst into the kitchen. "When do we eat? I'm starving!"

A sturdy seven-year-old, she had Mama's curly dark hair and brown eyes.

The hearty smell of roast chicken filled the house. "Supper is still an hour away," Mama said. "But you can have some crackers."

Leanne dashed to the pantry before Mama changed her mind. Mama turned back to me and helped me shell the peas. "What's my maiden name?"

"Schmidt," I said, "but Gramma and Grampa were born here."

"That's true, but *their* parents weren't."

"Your grandparents? I thought they were from Hungary."

"Darling, Hungary used to be part of Germany. They called it the Austro-Hungarian Empire. My *oma* and *opa* spoke German."

"You learned German from them?"

"They never learned English, so that was the only way we could talk to them."

"Who taught you?" Leanne piped up. I had forgotten she was in the room.

"Don't talk with your mouth full, Leanne," Mama chided. As Leanne chewed the cracker, a dusting of flakes coated her lips.

"Your grandfather used to sit me down every night. He'd get a children's book off the shelf next to the fireplace. We would go through it and translate. He'd make me pronounce all the words."

"What was the book?" I asked.

"I'll never forget it: *Struwwelpeter*."

"What does it mean in English?"

"It doesn't really translate. But the main character was called Peter. It was about all the bad things that happen to children when they misbehave." She looked over at Leanne, whose eyes grew as wide as half-dollars.

"What happened to them, Mama?" she said.

"I recall that there was a monster, and he had very long nails. As sharp as scissors."

"You better watch out, Leanne," I said.

"Oh, Mary-Catherine, there's no such things as monsters."

"Are you sure?" I teased.

Leanne looked at me, then at Mama. For a second I thought she was going to burst into tears.

I laughed. "I'm kidding, Leanne. There's no monster here."

Leanne ran to Mama and buried her head on her shoulder. Mama gazed at me and shook her head. I went back to the early peas I was shelling. I didn't know much about my mother's past. I knew how she met my father, of course, at a Christmas party in Chicago. How they fell in love and Dad joked about the risks of marriage between an Irishman and a Hungarian. How the joke was on him because they had close to a perfect marriage. But I didn't know as much as I wanted, I now realized.

I opened the oven door and basted the chicken. The poor old thing had been alive this morning.

"Mary-Catherine, there is one thing we need to discuss." Mama cleared her throat and stirred the potatoes. "You can't hobnob with the prisoners."

I felt my cheeks flame. Had she seen me wave to the German prisoner?

"Yes, I saw." She read my mind. "We are doing our patriotic duty while your father is away by letting these men work on our farm. And, of course, we are paying them for their help."

"They're getting paid?"

"Five dollars a day."

"That's a lot of money. We can afford it?"

Mama nodded. "It's only for two weeks. I've spoken to Mr. Skidmore at the bank. He's allowing me to borrow what we need. But that's not the point. There are rules. And we must follow them. One rule is not to talk about them when you go into town."

"Why not?"

"The army doesn't want people to get upset that they're here." She paused. "Although with so many of them around here, I'm not sure I understand their reasoning." She shook her head, then looked directly at me. "But rules are rules. Especially in wartime. The second rule is not to mingle with them."

I made a brushing aside gesture. "Mama, it was nothing."

"I don't trust them. And neither should you."

"You're just saying that because they're German."

"I saw the way he looked at you." She paused. "The sooner you take that job at the factory, the better. Right after harvest, you're moving to Chicago."

Harvest couldn't come soon enough. I couldn't wait to be free.

CHAPTER 4

Reinhard

Our dinner—or supper, as the farmers call it—was waiting for us when we returned to camp. Pork tonight, with mashed potatoes and cabbage. I would rather have cleaned up and sipped a glass of wine before eating, as I did back home, but that, of course, was out of the question.

I showered after dinner. It was to be a quiet evening until lights-out, so a few of us decided to play cards. Franz, Friedrich, and a young soldier who'd just arrived in camp joined us for skat. It turned out he was damn good. We talked between tricks. Johannes Kohl was from Leipzig. He'd been in Tunisia, in the Twenty-First also, operating a tank. He said he actually met Rommel.

I turned the conversation to the German-American Federation. Protests against the Nazi organization's leader, Fritz Kuhn, had been growing.

"They say the US is going to deport him." Franz shook his head.

"Too bad. At one point, the Bund was up to twenty thousand members."

Kohl was dummy this hand. He pulled out a cigarette. "Yah, but he is in prison. Embezzling money. What does that say about the man?"

I threw down my cards. "What do you mean?"

Kohl inhaled, the tip of his cigarette firing orange. He blew smoke in my direction.

"Do you believe everything the Jew newspapers tell you?" I said. "Fritz Kuhn is loyal to the Führer."

"Except that he stole nearly fifteen thousand dollars from the Bund," Kohl said.

"Are you a party member?" I asked.

Kohl cocked his head. "Is that important?"

"It is always important to know who one's allies are."

Kohl shrugged. "Kuhn is a fraud. Nothing more than a crook. A mobster. I hope he isn't one of *your* 'allies.'"

Franz jumped in. "Kuhn went to Germany and met the Führer in 'thirty-six."

"Does that make him less of a thief?"

Franz and I exchanged glances. I drew myself up. "I am Reinhard Deschler. My father was a *Zellenleiter* in Berlin. And I was a *Blockleiter.*"

Kohl grinned as he blew out smoke. "A lowly *Blockwart*, eh?"

Friedrich started laughing. When he saw my expression, he covered his mouth and turned the laugh into a cough.

"I am no snoop. I am proud to call myself an officer of the National Socialist Party." I let it sink in. "It appears you do not share that opinion."

Kohl flicked an ash onto the ground. "I've heard about people like you in these camps, Deschler." Then he stood up. "This tourney is over."

I called after him. "Wait."

Kohl slowed but didn't turn around.

"Be careful with whom you associate, Kohl. The war is not over."

Kohl didn't say anything for a moment. Then he spun around. "It is for us, you idiot." He paused for a moment, then clicked his heels, threw out his hand, and called out, "*Heil* Hitler."

Wilhelm

The heat that September night was stifling, the air as thick as the gravy on the mashed potatoes at supper. I tried to read on my cot, but sweat poured off me. Even the crickets outside were too hot to chirr. I closed my eyes, trying to ignore the scratchy blanket underneath, and thought of the breeze from the Danube River that danced across the fields on lazy late afternoons. When I was a boy, my parents would take me there on summer evenings to watch the day fade into evening. I remembered the trees bending gracefully, the breeze tickling their branches, as the water ruffled, then became as smooth as glass. How I missed Bavaria.

I was dozing when the new arrival, Johannes Kohl, stomped into the barracks. He brought with him the stench of cigarette smoke and body odor.

"What are you mad about?" I asked.

Ignoring me, he trudged across the room and threw himself on his cot.

I propped myself up on an elbow and slipped on my glasses. "Are you all right?"

His lips tightened, and he crossed his arms. He wasn't a tall man, but he was brawny and muscled. Sandy hair, a wide flat forehead, blue eyes, and a bristly mustache. A true Aryan.

"You are Stemm."

I nodded.

"What do you know about Deschler?"

I rolled over and sat up. "Reinhard?"

He grunted.

"He thinks we can still win the war. That anyone not loyal to the Führer is a spy for the Americans."

"Is that so?"

"He has his followers." I shrugged. "But I don't want trouble. I stay away from him. And you are draining the lagoons and don't have to work with him. He and I are on the same work detail. A farm. Helping with the harvest."

A wan smile flickered across Kohl's face. "Does everyone know everyone's business in this camp?"

"Of course."

He relaxed, and we started to chat. He was from Leipzig, not too far from me. We discovered an acquaintance or two in common. He was studying to be a doctor at university when he was conscripted. I was studying architecture.

"Ah. You and me. We are the same."

"How do you mean?"

"We are rational. Logical. That Deschler? He thinks he's better than us."

"True enough."

"He's a *Blockleiter. Mein Gott*, that's only a low-level official. He acts as if he were the Führer himself."

"As long as there is a Nazi Party, there will always be some who believe they are superior. The war is over."

"Try telling him that."

We were both quiet. Then he said, "You know, my neighbor in Munich was Jewish."

Why was he telling me this? I ran my tongue around my lips.

"She died in 'thirty-two. Cancer. Thank God. She didn't live to see"—he gestured—"everything that's happened."

CHAPTER 5

Wilhelm

Late last night a violent storm blasted through camp. Gale-force winds whipped the cabins; blue flashes of electricity crackled; thunder crashed. Sheets of rain gusted sideways, spilling through leaky windows and doors, soaking our bedding and pillows. I couldn't sleep, and most of the other prisoners were restless too. Then, just as quickly as it had come, it moved on. By morning, a meek and compliant sun rose as if nothing was amiss. The air smelled fresh and sweet. The only reminders of the storm were waterlogged ditches on the sides of the road.

We rolled up to the farm an hour after daybreak. Our task was to inspect the orchard and remove any damaged fruit before we picked it. It was backbreaking work, especially with little sleep. I was grateful when we stopped for lunch. The farmer's daughter, whose name was Mary-Catherine, I learned, brought out a tray of sandwiches, fruit, and lemonade. We relaxed under the shade of a giant elm in the front yard. Some of the men napped. Others ate their sandwiches slowly, as if one bite could stop time.

We were about to go back to work when we heard the swell of stringed music, followed by a touch of horns. A quiet bass paced the rhythm, and seconds later, a man began to sing. His voice was a silky light baritone, so light it could have been a tenor. But it was his style that captivated me. Slow, seductive, as clear as crystal. It was Frank Sinatra, the singer all the Americans—what am I saying? people all over the world—were crazy about.

I closed my eyes and allowed myself to be swept away. I didn't speak English, but it was easy to pick out the words "Night and Day," and I recognized the Cole Porter tune. How many times had I heard it in the cabarets and at my friend Richter Stein's? His parents had a phonograph and his mother used to say she loved Sinatra so much she might move to New Jersey, where he lived, to be closer to him. That was before the war, of course. Everything joyful was before. The cabarets, the music. The Steins. *Gott im Himmel* only knew if they were still alive.

I opened my eyes. The other men were listening too, some with their heads cocked to the side, eyes closed, smiles on their faces.

Then a clear pure soprano voice, at least two octaves above Sinatra's, joined in. She mimicked Sinatra's inflection. The same sense of yearning and seduction. Was it the mother or the daughter? I didn't know, but that anyone could sing with such abandon in the middle of a ghastly war was a miracle ... a tiny moment that suggested an end to the destruction, cruelty, and sorrow. The promise that we could one day sing again.

Mary-Catherine

After I made lunch for the prisoners—Spam sandwiches and apples from the orchards—I turned on the phonograph and finished dusting the living room to Sinatra's "Night and Day." Mama and Dad loved big band music and swing as much as I did. For me, it was a bittersweet experience. When I played Frank's music, I missed my Dad. He'd taught me how to jitterbug and how to appreciate Benny Goodman. He would roll up the rug in the living room and I would roll down my bobby sox, and we'd have a time of it until Mama came in, wondering what all the racket was. She'd take my place and I'd watch them glide across the room in perfect lockstep. I often wondered if I'd ever find a man as fun loving and kind as my father. It was hard to imagine him fighting—and maybe even killing—our enemies.

Once the song was over, I hung up my apron and decided to muck out the barn. But when I went outside, I stopped short. Most of the prisoners were still lounging on the lawn under the elm tree. Many wore dreamy expressions and smiled.

For an instant I wondered what could have caused them to look so happy. When I realized what it was, I felt a deep flush climb my neck. I had been singing out loud. I crept toward the barn, pulling up my bobby sox, wondering how I could ever face them again. Then one of the prisoners started to applaud. Another man joined in, then another, and before I knew it, all of them were clapping and whistling and calling out in German. I didn't understand them, but from their expressions, I knew they'd liked the song.

I smiled, straightened, and headed to the barn.

CHAPTER 6

Reinhard

After the girl sang I snuck a glance at the other prisoners. Most of them seemed stupefied, under a trance-like spell. No doubt they were thinking about home, peace, girls. It was enough to make me want to throttle them. Had they forgotten we were at war? America was our enemy. How could any German soldier be so feckless? They were close to treason by condoning this farm girl's singing.

I knew what she was doing. Dulling their senses, seducing them with song. What was next? Prying secrets out of them? Spying for the Allies? I sniffed. Wilhelm Stemm, Heinrich, and even Franz were applauding. Showering her with praise. It was hideous. Our mission wasn't over just because we were away from the battlefield. The Führer would be outraged. As was I.

I rose and dusted my hands on my pants. As I did, a wave of dizziness overpowered me, and I pitched forward. I collapsed on the ground, head spinning. I wanted to squeeze my eyes shut, but if I did, my head would spin more and I would undoubtedly vomit.

Damn the Allies! It was their fault. We'd been in North Africa, on a plain not far from the Cyrenaica desert: no landmarks, shade, or water. Frequent sandstorms blinded us, making us cough and spit up our guts. The sand stung our skin, our mouths, our teeth, any part of our bodies that was not covered. The flies were another scourge, making us sick with their venom. But we were considered an elite force, thanks to the leadership of Field Marshal Rommel.

During a skirmish we got too close to a British tank, but we didn't know it, and a cannonball narrowly missed us. The explosion shattered my eardrums. To this day I am almost deaf in one ear and subject to severe bouts of vertigo. When it hits, I am paralyzed. I cannot move, talk, or fight.

Franz saw me fall and ran over. "Reinhard?"

I couldn't reply. It would take too much effort to speak, and even the movement of my lips or eyes would bring on more spinning. I lay on the ground, not moving.

Franz called out. "Help! Deschler is down."

Two guards ran over. "What's going on?"

Franz explained.

"Why didn't we know this?" one of them said.

Franz shrugged. "Ask him." But I was in no position to reply.

"Well, crap." The pudgy guard looked around. "Stemm . . . and you . . ." He pointed to another prisoner. "Get over here. We need help."

Mary-Catherine

I was cleaning out Rosie's stall when they brought him into the barn. One man had his arms, the other his legs. They were flanked by the guards who drove the truck. A sudden fear skipped up my spine.

"Is there someplace we can put him down?" the pudgy guard asked, with as much emotion as if he was talking about a dog.

"What happened?"

"Apparently, he has a war injury," he said. He laid a finger on his own temple. "Vertigo. From an explosion in North Africa."

I nodded, still uneasy. I told him he could put the man down near the ladder to the loft. I spread an old blanket on the floor of the barn.

After they lowered him, the pudgy guard nodded to his partner, who turned to me. "Look," the skinny one said, "I know this isn't procedure, but we have to make sure the men get back to work. Can you handle him for a minute? He's not going anywhere."

I tensed. Me alone with a German prisoner? A Nazi? I wasn't supposed to talk to them, much less care for their injuries.

"He's pretty much out of it. He won't give you any trouble. If he does, just yell. We'll be back in two shakes of a lamb's tail."

I shifted and bit my lip. "Well, if it's only a minute or two."

"Thank you, little lady." The guards trotted out of the barn.

I studied the man on the floor, still clutching the shovel in my hand. Just in case. I needn't have. His face was so pale it looked blue. His eyes were closed, and he wasn't moving at all, except for the shallow rise and fall of his chest. He seemed as meek as a newborn calf. Still, I recognized him. He was the soldier who'd jumped down from the truck the first day they'd arrived. He'd waved to make sure I saw him, all sinewy muscle, straw-blond hair, and piercing blue eyes.

My stomach knotted, and I leaned the shovel against the stall. Should I keep mucking out the barn? Wait for the guards to come back? I rubbed a hand across my chin. What was the best course of action? The least dangerous?

As I was trying to decide, his eyes widened a crack, and I heard him groan. My heart skipped. I'd thought he was unconscious.

"You're awake."

Reinhard

I groaned. I would have spoken, but my head—indeed my entire body—felt like it was rotating around one those carousels on which children play. Thinking about moving my lips made my stomach roil. I slowly opened my eyes.

"You're awake," I heard a voice say. The girl.

I managed to lift a finger toward my mouth. "*Wasser*," I croaked.

She stared at me as if I had asked for the moon. Then she dipped her head, went to a wall in the barn, and lifted a bucket off a hook. She walked out. I heard the pump lever up and down, followed by the swish of running water.

She came back and brought the bucket close. She put it down and held up her index finger, as if signaling me to wait. I scoffed inwardly. Where was I going to go? She scrounged around the barn and came up with a small tin container. She carefully poured water into it and brought it to my lips. I struggled to sit up, and she seemed to understand. She lifted my head and gave me a drink. I took a few sips, then closed my eyes to indicate I was done.

She relaxed her hold on my neck and lowered my head. I

blinked my thanks. The vertigo started to subside, but I decided no one needed to know that.

I sighed. "*Gut*," I croaked. "*Danke.*"

"You're welcome." A tiny smile curled her lips.

I reached up and clasped her hand, the one still behind my neck. "*Schön.*"

CHAPTER 7

Mary-Catherine

I had never been that close to a German soldier. I had never been that close to any man, except Steve. To Steve I was a girl. This man, though—even half-conscious, I'd never been looked at the way he looked at me. I could tell he saw me as a woman. A desirable one. It happened when he reached for my hand. I wasn't prepared for it, and for an instant, it was a shock. But then I felt his cool fingers, the firm skin of his palm. And something else, too. I couldn't explain it, but I felt as if a jolt of energy had jumped into my hand. We were connected in some secret way.

I smiled in spite of myself and looked into his eyes. He was watching me, his expression intense. Registering every pore, every hair on my head. I swallowed. I should get up. Go back into the house. I was breaking the rules. But I wanted to stay.

It was then the pudgy guard came back and saw that the prisoner's eyes were open. "You better, Deschler?"

I scrambled to my feet. Deschler. Was that his first name? Or his last?

He groaned. "A little."

He spoke English! Thickly accented, but still . . .

The plump guard turned to me. "I'll get him into the truck. He can rest there. Thanks again, missy. You helped us out."

I watched as the guard pulled him up. A moan escaped the prisoner's lips. Real or false? The guard draped his arm around Deschler's shoulder and helped him walk out of the barn. Deschler looked dazed. At the last minute, though, before they turned the corner, he said, "Thank you, Mary-Catherine. I am Reinhard."

My mouth fell open. How did he know my name? Why had he told me his?

I did the rest of my chores in a fog. Reinhard was a foreigner. A German, for God's sake. Our enemy. Not only was he dangerous, but I wasn't supposed to associate with him. Still. There was something about him. I'd felt it when we first laid eyes on each other. And then when he reached for my hand. I wanted to know what it was. I needed to find out what it was.

● ● ●

That evening I was peeling carrots for stew, puzzling over what he'd said just before the guard came back into the barn. He'd said "*schön*." What did that mean?

I waited until we were washing up after supper. "Mama, I have a question."

"Sure."

"What does '*schön*' mean?"

Her reply was sharp. "Why?"

I shrugged. "I heard one of the prisoners say it. He looked over as if I knew what it meant." It wasn't altogether a lie.

She planted her hands on her hips. "Who? When?"

I tightened my lips. "It was after lunch," I lied. "I was bringing in the trays, and I had Frank Sinatra on the phonograph. One of the soldiers snapped his fingers and after 'Night and Day,' he said, '*Schön*.'"

She raised her chin. "Ahh." She relaxed. "I don't blame him. It means 'beautiful.'"

"Really?" I felt my cheeks get hot.

"Yes, and who doesn't think Sinatra is beautiful, German or not?"

I smiled.

"But what are you doing that you're close enough to overhear their conversation?" She waggled a finger. "They may be good workers, but they are our enemy. Never forget that."

That night I couldn't sleep. I tossed and turned, replaying our time in the barn until it was permanently engraved on my brain. I couldn't wait until tomorrow.

Wilhelm

Deschler was taken to the infirmary when we returned to camp, but the news spread quickly. Some of the men were sympathetic, recounting incidents about soldiers with shell shock. Others were more skeptical. Especially Kohl. We finished dinner and were smoking outside the barracks. A rosy sunset glittered through the trees, coating the leaves with a golden-red sheen. A reminder that autumn was not far off.

"So he was in the barn with the girl? Alone?"

I nodded.

Kohl snorted. "That's a problem."

"How?" I asked.

"The war didn't end for some just because they're no longer on the battlefield."

I cocked my head. "What do you mean?"

"Do you remember when you said Deschler was accusing everyone of spying for the Americans?"

I nodded.

"Well, it works the other way as well. It's said that some German prisoners are trying to collect whatever information they can about America and the US military for Germany."

"Are you saying Deschler is a German spy?"

Kohl took a deep drag. "If I saw a German soldier cozying up to an American, I would be suspicious."

I shook my head. "But that's just as absurd as *his* crazy accusations!"

"Is it?"

"What can Deschler get from a farm girl? She knows less about the US Army than we do." I tapped ash on the ground.

"Didn't you say her father is fighting in the Pacific?"

"That's what the guards told us. So?"

"There may be information we don't know. Hell, there could be information *she* doesn't even know she knows."

"From whom? About what?"

Kohl stubbed out his cigarette on the ground. "Didn't you say her mother speaks German?"

"Yah, but that doesn't mean she's a spy."

"Who knows? I just think you should keep an eye on them all. Especially Deschler. They could be setting up some kind of code."

"Really, Kohl."

"Look. You know the guy. He considers every American either an enemy or an asset. And then there's that nonsense in the barn . . . " He fished out another cigarette, eyed it as if weighing whether he really wanted it, then slipped it back into the package.

"Are you saying he faked his vertigo just to be alone with the girl?"

"Like I said, just keep your eye on him, Stemm. You're with him all day."

I flicked my cigarette onto the ground. I wasn't sure who was worse, Kohl or Deschler.

CHAPTER 8

Wilhelm

Deschler didn't come with us the next morning. The army called in a local doctor, who reportedly told him vertigo comes on quickly but leaves slowly. Although Deschler claimed to be feeling better, the doctor told him to take it easy. The camp commander echoed the doctor. In light of the Geneva Convention, no one wanted a sick German soldier. And Reinhard was the type to complain of cruel or unusual punishment.

We arrived at the farm at dawn. The sun hadn't yet made an appearance, and objects were still sliding out from the shadows. Thirty minutes later the two younger children came outside, neatly dressed and carrying lunch pails. Of course. It was September. School had begun. A few minutes later Mary-Catherine emerged with her mother. They chatted quietly, Mary-Catherine nodding. The mother clutched a purse, and keys dangled from her other hand. She was going to drive them to school in the old black coupe parked behind the barn. She was probably telling Mary-Catherine what to do in her absence.

The sun finally came out, warming the cool morning. We picked apples; I was one of two men assigned to haul the baskets from the orchard back to the barn.

As I made my first trip with the baskets, Mary-Catherine's gaze swept over me as though she was looking for someone. When she didn't see him, she tightened her lips. When she saw me watching her, she flushed and hurried back inside.

After lunch, I took my time walking back to the orchard. Lingering by the barn, I took off my glasses and wiped them on my shirt. As I put them back on, I spotted her coming toward me. I nodded politely. She nodded but kept walking until she'd reached the barn. Then she stopped and turned around.

"Do you speak English?"

"A little." I held my index finger and thumb close together. I wondered why she was asking.

"Just a little?"

I nodded.

"What's your name?"

"Stemm. Wilhelm Stemm."

She smiled. "Hello, Wilhelm."

I could feel myself color. What was this about?

"I remember you. I pointed you out to Harley last week."

I frowned, not understanding.

"Those." She gestured to my glasses. "My brother wears them, too. He had scarlet fever when he was a baby." She bit her lip. "I don't know how to say that in German. *Deutsch.*"

I flipped up my hands. I wasn't sure what she was saying.

Her gaze darted around the barn as if the answer to our

language impasse might be hanging on the wall. Then she focused on me.

"Wilhelm?" She smiled. With full lips, white teeth, rosy skin that looked as soft as lamb's wool, and those deep blue eyes, she looked lovely. "Reinhard?" she said. "He is okay? Yah?"

My spirits sank. I wanted to tell her he was dead. Or that he'd been transferred to another camp. I saw her first. And she me. But of course, she had never really *seen* me. Just my glasses. I looked down and hesitated. Truth or deception? Finally, I said, "Okay. Okay. *Nur ruhen. Morgen hier.*"

"*Morgen?*"

I wracked my brain. How did one translate "tomorrow"?

"He's coming back?"

"Yah. *Morgen.*"

Suddenly her face lit. "Tomorrow."

"Yah. Toomahrow."

"*Danke*, Wilhelm. *Danke.*" Her smile was melted sunshine. Then she disappeared into the barn.

● ● ●

The first thing I did when I got back to camp was hurry to the commissary. There was one German-English dictionary left, but I didn't have enough money to buy it. We earned five dollars a day, but the army took almost all of it to pay for our housing, food, and clothes. The dictionary cost a dollar—all I had was fifty cents. But the GI behind the counter took pity on me, or else he was thrilled I wanted to learn English, because he held a finger to his lips and gave it to me for half price. "Don't tell anyone."

I bowed my thanks and whispered, "*Stille.*"

In the barracks I pulled out a copy of *Steppenwolf* by Hermann

Hesse, one of our most famous authors. I'd read it at university before I decided to focus on architecture. The story is about Harry Haller, a man who feels alienated from bourgeois society and is often suicidal. Eventually he meets a woman who introduces him to sex and drugs, although it turns out she may not have been real at all. The story is about Haller's inner struggle, and most of the time, he is in despair. Perhaps even insane.

It was the theme of my generation. After the Great War, Germany struggled. The economy was out of control; it was impossible to make ends meet. Why shouldn't we feel despair? Of course, Hitler and the National Socialists claimed they were the solution, and things did get better. For a little while. Eventually, though, the solution proved to be worse than the problem.

I picked up the dictionary, opened *Steppenwolf*, and started to translate words here and there. I wrote them down. Then I tried to pronounce them with that flat, wide-open American accent. I needed to learn English.

Reinhard

They released me from the infirmary around suppertime, once they were convinced my head was no longer spinning like a top. I went back to my barracks, which housed almost fifty men. But the only one inside was Stemm. He looked up at me, raised his brows, then went back to whatever he was doing.

I watched him for a few seconds. "What are you doing?"

"Reading," Stemm said after a pause.

"With that?" I pointed to the dictionary.

"I thought I'd try to teach myself some English."

"You didn't study it at university?"

"Yes, but I haven't practiced in months."

"Why bother? We'll be home soon. Some people could see it as disloyalty."

Stemm stared at me as though he thought I was joking.

"And even if we're not home soon, I wouldn't give the Americans the satisfaction of learning their language."

"Easy to say when your English is better than mine."

I shrugged. Of course it was. But you never knew when it would present an opportunity. As it might with that farm girl. "I would only speak it if it was to my advantage." I paused. "We know who is a loyal Nazi and who is not." I clicked my heels and straightened my arm. "*Heil* Hitler."

CHAPTER 9

———

Mary-Catherine

The next morning I wolfed down breakfast so I could go outside and watch the prisoners arrive. When I saw Reinhard on the truck, my face felt like it was on fire. He saw me too and smiled like the sneaky cat who has stolen the cream. Goose bumps ran up my arms.

Mama came outside. She was going to do some errands after she took the kids to school. Then she was going to visit her aunt, who lived in Park Ridge. She wouldn't be back until school let out. I was in charge. She listed the chores I needed to do.

I washed the breakfast dishes, made the beds, swept the floor. I tried to focus on my work. I really did. But I kept remembering Reinhard's pale eyes. His straight blond hair. Every second I didn't see him or know what he was doing felt like an hour. I longed for him in a way I never had for Steve.

Oh yes, Steve and I had been lovers, and at the time, I thought he'd be the only one. I was his first, too, and our clumsy efforts made me wonder what all the fuss was about. But I was two years older now, and what I felt for Reinhard was very different.

That morning my senses were heightened. Every time my fingers brushed an object, I could feel its shape, its texture, its weight. Whether it was the wall or the broom handle or the sheets on the bed, I sensed rough surfaces, smooth wood, or cool silkiness. My hearing was sharper, too. I was sure I heard the whisper of the breeze, the insects buzzing in the fields, maybe even thoughts riffling through people's minds. I was Superman with X-ray vision and super hearing. The worst part—or the best, depending on your perspective—was that I was no longer afraid. I knew I was supposed to feel shame. Mine weren't the thoughts of a "nice" girl. But I didn't feel any guilt. The war had turned everything topsy-turvy. When you don't know whether your father or brother or boyfriend will still be alive afterward, it's easy to live in the moment.

When it was time to prepare the prisoners' lunch, I could hardly wait to see him. I threw together a plate of sandwiches, some with peanut butter and jelly, some with Spam and mustard. I made a pitcher of iced tea and hurried everything out to the front yard.

He'd been waiting. I could tell by the look in his eyes. As I served the sandwiches and he reached to get his, he said quietly, "Good day, *Fraulein*."

I dipped my head.

"I cannot stop thinking about you," he whispered.

My breath caught.

"You have put a spell over me."

I stepped back, so startled I almost dropped the pitcher of tea. That was exactly what *he* had done to *me*. My pulse thumped. I was sure I was trembling. He was so close I could smell his sweat. And something else. Pomade?

"*Fraulein*, will you do me the honor and meet me in the barn during our afternoon break?" He shot me a meaningful look.

I swallowed. Nodded. I didn't trust myself to speak.

• • •

Two hours later, just before they took a break, I ran upstairs and changed from jeans into a dress. Lipstick was in short supply during the war, and I never wore it. But today, I sneaked into Mama's room and borrowed the tube of Brave Scarlet I'd seen her apply on special occasions. I ran a brush through my hair and smoothed my dress. I turned around, ready to go back downstairs. Then I stopped, went back to her bureau, and opened the top drawer. A small bottle of Chanel No. 5 lay inside; it was the only perfume she ever wore. I carefully dabbed a drop on my throat and my wrists.

Then I took the stairs down. I could see the men wander in from the orchard. I went outside and headed toward the barn.

CHAPTER 10

Mary-Catherine

Reinhard was waiting for me by one of the stalls. When I entered, his eyes widened.

I smiled.

He took a step forward, then stopped. "I will close the doors." He inclined his head in their direction.

I hesitated for an instant. We didn't have much time. Or privacy. Then I nodded.

He went to the doors and closed them. "One of the guards is sick today. We should have time." He came back and stood in front of me. "Have you been thinking about me?"

I cleared my throat. I couldn't answer.

He smiled. "You have. I can tell."

I looked into his eyes. My stomach flipped. I felt as if he had suddenly grown as large as one of those circus lions and was about to swallow me whole.

He read my mind. "You are afraid?"

I didn't reply. He should only know I was more eager than fearful.

He pulled me back into one of the stalls. He lifted my chin, then leaned in and kissed me. It was long, slow, and deep. Steve and I used to make out in the toolshed, but our sessions were nothing like this. This was the kiss I'd heard about in the romance magazines my girlfriends giggled over. The kiss that makes you tingle and sends a quiver down your back.

His kisses grew harder. Almost demanding. I drank him in, trying to give back what I got. The fact that it was forbidden made it irresistible. He groaned and pulled me against him in a tight hold. He was hard. With Steve it was a signal for me to lie down in the backseat of his car, at the edge of the orchard, or wherever we were, for a brief moment of fumbling and eventual release. But now I didn't move.

Breathing hard, he started to take off his pants. I wanted him—so much—but this wasn't the place. The barn wasn't private enough. And even with one guard sick, a prisoner might notice he was gone and start asking questions. I don't know how I mustered the strength, but I stretched out my arms and pushed him away. "No!" I cried.

His eyes narrowed and grew cold. "What do you mean, no?" His voice was sharp, as if annoyed. He started toward me again.

"Not here." I took a step back. "What if someone barges in?" I looked at him. "I know a better place. Tomorrow. Same time."

Wilhelm

I was near the front of the house when I saw them walk out of the barn. They didn't notice me. First Reinhard crept out, wearing a smug look. He adjusted his pants, as if he'd just done his business. A burst of anger shot through me. He sauntered back to the orchard. A moment later Mary-Catherine came out, her cheeks bright red. She kept smoothing down her dress. My pulse started to race.

I forced myself to hold my tongue for the rest of the day, but that evening back at camp, I couldn't stay silent. I had to let Reinhard know what I'd seen. I would be subtle, frame it as a warning. At least that's what I told myself. We knew it was *verboten* to mingle with the Americans. The penalty was harsh—any soldier caught would be locked up for the duration of the war. Was Reinhard willing to risk spending the rest of his time in the stockade?

I walked up to him outside the mess tent after dinner. "A moment, Reinhard."

He spun around. "Yes?" He was a few inches taller than I. He drew himself up as if to emphasize the difference.

"You need to be careful."

He scowled. "Whatever are you talking about, Stemm?"

"Mary-Catherine."

He didn't reply for a moment, but I saw several emotions unfold across his face. The first was fear, as if he'd never considered that his behavior had been witnessed. Then came a concentrated frown with furrowed brows, as if he was debating how to reply. Finally, the familiar haughty glare returned, and his brows arched. "The stupid farm girl?"

I nodded. I wanted to punch him for calling her stupid.

He snorted. "I don't know what you are talking about, Stemm. She's a cow. Ugly. Rudimentary."

I let out an angry breath. "She fancies you. I saw you come out of the barn this afternoon. You could be in big trouble if anyone finds out."

"And you'll be the one to sound the alarm, won't you, Stemm."

"Do you really think that little of me, Deschler?" I fisted my hands. It took all my resolve to keep them at my sides. "We are only at the farm for another week or so. Are a few days of seduction worth spending the rest of the war locked up?"

He stared at me with suspicion. "I know what you're doing. You want her for yourself. It's been obvious since the day we first arrived. But she couldn't care less about you." He let out a smug laugh. "She's mine, Stemm. Mine."

I tightened my lips and stayed quiet until I composed myself. "Your vertigo has made you delusional, Deschler. If you persist, your problems will be much more serious than trying to humiliate me."

He glared at me. "If it becomes public, I'll know who leaked it."

I shrugged. "You know I would never turn on a fellow soldier." I started to walk away. "Just remember I tried to warn you."

Neither of us knew then that Kohl was nearby, listening to every word.

CHAPTER 11

Mary-Catherine

It was another hot night, especially for September, and I couldn't sleep. But, truth be told, even if it had been in January, I would have been awake. I was so restless I bunched the sheets with my feet. I lay in the dark, hoping the night breeze would cool me, but it was no use. I couldn't think about anyone or anything except Reinhard and the way he made me feel. What I wanted was immoral and wrong. I wanted it anyway. It wouldn't be a sin, would it, if no one knew? But I had to move fast. The prisoners would be here for only another week. I didn't want to waste a single day.

The next morning Mama made pancakes, but I wasn't hungry. I just sat at the table drinking Postum. Mama looked at me curiously. "Is anything the matter, Mary-Catherine? You look a little peaked."

I shook my head. "Couldn't sleep."

She nodded. "I was awake too." An irrational pang of fear ran through me. Could she hear me tossing and turning? Did she somehow know?

"Why were you awake?"

Her answer reassured me. "Even with help from the prisoners, I'm afraid we're going to have a lean harvest." She sighed. "Well below what we usually take in. The only thing that helps is that prices are up."

A momentary shame rolled over me. Here I was thinking about a man, and she was trying to provide for the family. Still, I couldn't help resenting the fact that I couldn't dwell on Reinhard. It was the war, of course. It changed everything. Even our innermost thoughts. Good thing I was leaving after harvest. The sooner I moved to Chicago, the better.

"What can I do?"

She smiled, a little sadly, I thought. "Just what you've been doing, my sweet. We'll manage. Somehow." She looked through the window out at the fields. "We'll have to do more canning this season. Perhaps sell applesauce and preserves at the farmers' market. That could help." She chewed absentmindedly on her nail. "In fact, would you round up the canning jars and wash them out? I think they're in the toolshed."

I straightened. Was this a trick? The toolshed was exactly where I would meet Reinhard later today. I looked over at Mama, but she was still gazing out the window.

• • •

The toolshed, obscured by a stand of aspens, sat at the back of our property. I hadn't been inside in months, and when I opened the door, the faint stench of skunk told me the critters had found a way in and had been using it as a brothel. I remembered when

Dad built it. He'd deliberately made the height less than six feet, saying it was more like a pantry or closet than a real shed. Shelves cornered on three sides, and there wasn't much more space. When I was a little girl, this was my favorite spot for hide-and-seek. Leanne and Harley carried on the tradition, but spiderwebs in the corners indicated they must have found a new hidey-hole. Like I said, the war changed everything, even the games children played. Now they played "Allies and Axis."

I skirted the tiny paw prints on the dirt floor and looked for the Mason jars. I spotted some in a box on the top shelf, crammed between blades for Dad's saw and a bunch of small baskets. There were dozens of jars, but we'd need still more if Mama was serious about canning.

Nonetheless, I slid a box of jars to the edge of the shelf, balanced them carefully in my arms, and stowed them outside the shed door. I'd have to carry the rest out and wash them all, but that could wait until later. I rummaged around and found a broom. I tried to sweep the floor but stopped when I realized I was just pushing the dirt around. A scratchy old blanket lay folded up in a corner. I retrieved it, thanked my lucky stars it was there, and spread it on the floor.

Reinhard

When it was time for our break, I climbed down from the ladder on which I'd been perched and pointedly covered my forehead with my hand. I squeezed my eyes shut and leaned against the ladder for support.

The skinny guard noticed. "What's the problem, Deschler?"

"I—I think I'm getting vertigo again."

I peeked out. The guard's eyes narrowed; he was clearly unsure whether to believe me.

At that moment, Franz ran up, as I'd asked him to. "This is serious," he said to the guard. "If Deschler has another bout of it …" He let his voice trail off as I'd instructed. I almost smiled, ready to say, "Well done," but managed to keep my mouth closed.

The guard was still suspicious, but he had been trained to treat us well, especially in matters pertaining to our health.

"I think if I could rest for an hour, things might settle down," I said.

He sighed. "Go back to the truck. You can rest in the bed. I'll be up in a few minutes."

"Perhaps I will take a walk. Sometimes that restores my balance."

The guard shook his head. "No way. You stay in the truck where I can see you."

I nodded. I had no intention of obeying. In fact, I took a calculated risk that he wouldn't be able to see me if I was lying prone in the bed of the truck. He just hadn't figured it out. I guessed I had about thirty minutes.

I meandered out of the orchard. Mary-Catherine had told me where the toolshed was in relation to the barn. I headed toward it, circled behind, and trotted over to a stand of trees in a corner of the property.

She was inside, of course, waiting for me, but my spirits sank. This was not a suitable place for a tryst. It was dirty and musty and smelled like skunk. But then I made myself rally. What choice did I have? The opportunity she presented could be huge. I forced a smile.

She smiled back and came toward me. I knew what she wanted.

But first I would show her who was boss. As we embraced, I pushed her dress up and shoved her to the floor. She seemed startled but followed my lead. Moments later I squeezed her breasts and thrust myself inside her. I heard her yelp. Was she a virgin? She couldn't be. The girls—or should I say the women—I'd been with at home weren't. Just to be safe, though, I covered her mouth with my hand. "Be quiet," I muttered. "Someone will hear. The pain will stop."

And it did. In a few minutes she arched herself upward and let me do what I wanted. After it was over, she lay next to me. Her face was smeared with dirt and grime, but she wore a silly grin. I couldn't help myself. I smiled back.

She was mine.

CHAPTER 12

Mary-Catherine

We met again in the toolshed the next afternoon. Reinhard drew me to him. His hands roamed my breasts.

"I must have you." He sounded almost hoarse.

"I want you, too," I whispered. I couldn't help myself. I knew it was forbidden love. That to make friends with, not to mention make love to, the enemy in war was tantamount to treason. My family would never accept it. But Reinhard was different. I loved him. And he loved me. Didn't that give us a pass?

Afterward, as I lay in his arms, I said, "I want to tell the whole world about you. I never thought I would fall in—"

He cut me off. "Love?" His tone was curt. Biting. But then he backed down as if he knew he'd been cruel. "I cannot think of anyone else either."

I wriggled closer and draped my arm over his chest. I didn't speak for a moment. "There's a problem," I finally said.

He scowled. "What is that?"

"I'm supposed to leave the farm at the end of harvest season. I won't be able to see you."

He raised himself onto an elbow. "Where are you going?"

"To Chicago to work a factory job." I laughed. "Just like Rosie the Riveter."

"Who?"

I shook my head. "Never mind."

But his eyes sparked with interest. "Where will you live?"

"In a rooming house for young women. On the southeast side of Chicago. Near Republic Steel, which is where I will be working."

He inclined his head.

"Yes. You should come and visit. When you are free."

"I will be returning to Germany."

"No!" I exclaimed. "How will we see each other? Just when we finally . . ."

He held a finger against my lips. "We will find a way. Meanwhile, we have today. And tomorrow. And, hopefully, the day after." He hesitated. "Mary-Catherine, will you do something for me?"

"Anything." I tried to kiss his finger but a crick in the back of my neck from the awkward way I'd been lying made me lift a hand to rub it. As I did, frantic shouts from outside sent a bolt of fear through me. I froze, my hand in midair.

Reinhard never told me what he wanted. In fact, a look of panic streaked across his face. "*Scheisse!* What will we do?"

I squeezed my eyes shut in concentration. Then I sprang into action. I jumped up and began to button my dress. "We'll be fine. But you must do exactly what I say."

Wilhelm

Late September afternoons in America are not that different from those in Germany. The sun tried its best to cover us with a blanket of warmth, but the nip in the air signaled that our balmy days, like a candle whose flame would soon be extinguished, were numbered.

The guards called for a water break, and we trudged to the pump in front of the farmhouse, leaving our baskets and ladders in the orchard. This was our second and final week at the farm, but there was plenty of work yet to do. We had harvested a lot of the apples, but more than half the trees were still laden with fruit. I guessed that by the end of the week we would have picked and sorted half of what remained. The rest would wither and rot of its own accord. Even with our labor it would not be a bountiful harvest for the family.

We took turns yanking the lever on the pump. I had just poured water over my head and straightened to let it drip down my neck when I realized I hadn't seen Deschler or Mary-Catherine for the better part of an hour. Deschler had been complaining of his vertigo again, and the guards had allowed him to rest in the bed of the truck. I edged over and looked in the vehicle. No Deschler.

I stiffened. I faced a dilemma. Should I go to the guards with my suspicions? That would risk Deschler's wrath. He would claim I was wrong. That I was nothing but a troublemaker. He'd say that I was jealous. He might even pick a fight with me when we got back to camp. Have Franz beat me so badly I'd end up in the infirmary.

But what roiled my gut was that he had put the rest of us in jeopardy. If he was gone, playing a prank, or, most likely, holed up with Mary-Catherine, we would all be punished. We'd be confined to camp, our privileges rescinded, and the fragile tendrils of trust built between prisoners and guards destroyed. For all I knew, we might all end up in the stockade.

My only choice was to say nothing. I didn't want to get Mary-Catherine or the other prisoners in trouble. And Deschler was right about one thing. I *was* jealous. The man had no special charms, and he clearly lacked compassion for—or interest in—anyone except himself. Indeed, I questioned what kind of girl Mary-Catherine must be, to be so enamored of a lizard. To be so attracted that she would risk her reputation, perhaps even her safety, for a few stolen kisses. I bit my lip and trudged back to the pump.

An old yellow school bus clattered down the road. It shuddered to a stop in front of the farmhouse, and the two O'Rourke children hopped off. The little girl went straight inside, but the boy . . . what was his name? Harley—that was it—trotted over to the barn and poked his head inside. He was probably looking for Mary-Catherine since Mrs. O'Rourke wouldn't be home until supper.

Seconds later Harley came out. He obviously hadn't seen Mary-Catherine, but he didn't seem upset. His glasses slipped, and he pushed them back up his nose and wandered toward the orchard.

The guards told us break was over and did a head count. They frowned. Someone was missing. We prisoners eyed one another, as if reluctant to admit who it was, though I guessed we all knew.

Finally, one of the guards said, "Deschler. He's not here."

The skinny guard nodded and called over to the truck. "Deschler, nap time is over. Get into formation."

Nothing happened. The guard yelled in a louder voice. "Deschler. Let's go."

Still nothing.

The guard let out an annoyed breath, went to the truck, and peered in. When he returned to us, his hand hovered over the revolver holstered at his waist.

"All right. Where is he?"

We looked at one another, still reluctant to speak. I wondered how such a nasty bully as Deschler had so much sway over us. Was it because he was an ardent Nazi who strutted around as if he was the Führer himself? Did the men really believe we would still overcome the Allies? With our forces retreating on all fronts? No one answered. Finally, I piped up.

"I might know," I said quietly.

The tall, skinny guard wheeled around. "Well?" he said in a gruff, impatient tone. As though I was the guilty one, not Deschler.

I turned in the direction of the shed and motioned for the guard to follow. We started off, but all at once, we heard a high-pitched scream, a crash, and a loud *thwack*. It came from the direction of the orchard. All of us spun around, guards and prisoners alike, and sprinted to the orchard.

The ladder was lying on the ground on its side. One of the baskets was upside down, apples spilled all over the ground. In the middle of the mess sprawled Harley. Blood seeped out of his nose, and his legs were twisted into unnatural angles. He lay still, eyes shut, his eyeglasses a few feet away. The lenses glinted in the sun.

CHAPTER 13

————

Wilhelm

Chaos ensued. Men shouted, and several prisoners ran back to the pump for water, although what that would do was unclear. Two others searched for a stiff board. The others formed a tight knot around the boy. One of the guards gently slapped Harley's cheeks trying to revive him. Because his legs were not where they were supposed to be in relation to his torso, we suspected they were both broken.

"He must have climbed up the ladder," someone said.

"Maybe he was trying to swing up into the tree," another said. "You know how boys love to climb."

"Yes, but his eyes—those glasses . . ." A third man pointed to the specs on the ground. "They must have fallen off."

Yet another prisoner nodded. "He couldn't see, and he missed the branch."

"He needs to be in hospital," I said. "Right away."

"Where is his sister?" the pudgy guard said.

"Inside the house."

"No. The older one."

No one answered.

The guard turned to me. "Do you know where she is, Stemm?"

I was suddenly wary. I swallowed hard. Then I nodded.

"You stay with the boy," the guard hurriedly said to the prisoners surrounding Harley. "Keep trying to wake him." He waved to another man. "You go inside, tell the little girl to call for help. Then bring down a blanket, some ice, and rags." He pointed to another prisoner, who spoke English better than most of us. "You go, too, and translate. The rest of you"—he swept his hand toward me—"come."

Urgency replaced shock, and we split up to follow the guard's orders. The guard turned to me. "So, where is she?"

I motioned for him to follow and backtracked to the barn. Although I knew she wasn't inside, I suggested they call out her name. "It's Mary-Catherine."

The prisoners with us tried, but their thick accents made her name unintelligible. The American guard shook his head and bellowed, "Mary-Catherine . . . Miss O'Rourke. Where are you? There's an emergency!"

No response. I went behind the barn down to the stand of trees at the edge of the property. Earlier I'd seen a flash of her gingham dress through the branches. I stopped a respectable distance away and gestured toward the shed.

The guard called out. "Miss O'Rourke! Mary-Catherine! Come quickly! There's been an accident!" The other prisoners chimed in, and a cacophony of voices followed.

• • •

By the time Mary-Catherine appeared at the edge of the trees and moved toward us, her cheeks were red, and she was out of breath. Behind her was Deschler, carrying several trays of what looked like glass jars. He was flushed, too. When they saw us, Mary-Catherine cocked her head. Deschler looked down, refusing to make eye contact.

I stared at them, knowing what they'd been doing in the shed. It wasn't moving glass jars. Their high color and Reinhard's apparent unease were proof. I bit my lip, both angry and jealous, yet curious how they'd come up with the ruse. It had to be Reinhard; Mary-Catherine wasn't capable of deceit, was she? I didn't have much time to ponder it, though, because the pudgy guard scowled. For the first time, he looked as menacing as a wild dog. His lips thinned into a cold, hard line, as if he was on the verge of an inquisition. Then he let out a harsh breath.

Mary-Catherine froze. Her brows furrowed into what I took to be a worried but innocent expression. "What's going on? Why are you here?"

The guard ran his tongue around his lips, as if confused. "Come quickly, Miss O'Rourke. Your brother is hurt."

CHAPTER 14

Wilhelm

We didn't get back to camp until after dark. Everyone seemed shaken, even though the boy regained consciousness soon afterward. But that turned out to be a mixed blessing. As soon as his brain registered where he was and what had happened, he began to shriek, most likely in pain, tears of agony streaming down his cheeks. Mary-Catherine cried too, her beautiful blue eyes turning swollen and red. To her credit, she never left his side and tenderly stroked his forehead, whispering words of comfort until an ambulance arrived from Highland Park. She piled into the back and told Leanne to go to the neighbors' farm until her mother came home.

The guards said we'd babysit the little girl, but Mary-Catherine shook her head. Still, we remained at the farm until Mrs. O'Rourke returned. She arrived just before dusk. When the guards told her what had happened, her face went white and she sagged against the porch.

"Where is he?"

"The ambulance took him to Evanston Hospital. Your daughter is with him."

"And Leanne? My youngest?"

"At the neighbors'."

She ran back to her car, gunned the engine, and shot out of the driveway. After that we were loaded onto the truck, where we joined Deschler, who had been shackled a moment after he emerged from the shed. No one spoke on the ride back.

Mary-Catherine

Harley went into surgery right away. When he emerged, his legs were in traction, elevated and swathed in plaster casts. Luckily, he was still unconscious. I wished he could stay that way until his legs healed to avoid the pain I knew was coming. As they wheeled him into recovery, Mama arrived. She questioned me about what had happened. I told her the truth: that I was in the shed collecting the Mason jars for applesauce. I had asked one of the prisoners to help me because there were so many and they were so heavy.

"You asked a German to help you? What did I tell you about—"

I cut her off. "Mama, what was I supposed to do? There were close to seven dozen jars. I couldn't carry them by myself. Isn't that what they're here for?"

Her nostrils flared, and she stared at me with an expression that said she didn't believe me. I was about to repeat my story when the door to the visitors' area opened, and the surgeon came in to assure us that Harley would eventually be fine. He'd had a nasty fall, but with enough healing and the right exercises, he would be as right as rain.

"How did it happen?" he asked.

Mama glared at me.

"I was in the shed. Away from the orchard. And the prisoners were on break. I—"

The doctor frowned, "What prisoners?"

We explained.

"I had no idea. Real Jerries?" His eyes went wide with surprise. "I've heard rumors. So they're true?"

I nodded. "Anyway, I was collecting Mason jars from our shed and asked one of the prisoners to help me carry them to the pump so I could wash them. Harley and Leanne had been dropped off after school, and apparently, no one noticed him stealing down to the orchard. The ladder was right there, so I suppose he decided it was time for him to climb one of the trees. Unfortunately—"

Mama cut in. "Harley has very bad eyesight. He's worn glasses since he was a little boy. He must have missed the branch . . ." She glared in my direction. "At least that's what I understand."

"You weren't there?"

"No. As my daughter says, she was in the shed getting Mason jars for canning. I was in town doing errands."

The doctor nodded. "Ah, well, I am sorry. He's going to have a few bad weeks. Best he stays here during that time."

Mama spoke up. "Doctor, I appreciate your concern, but—the cost—we are not rich. We are simple farmers. My husband is in the Pacific."

"I am aware there is a war going on," the doctor said. He opened his mouth, about to say something, but then closed it, apparently changing his mind. Then he said, "We'll work it out. Don't worry. We'll take good care of your son."

CHAPTER 15

Reinhard

Back at camp, I was thrown into the stockade. A rough-hewn wood hut, it squatted near the back of the camp property. Most of the other buildings, including the barracks and mess hall, were built to house workers during the American Depression, but the jail was a new addition. It wasn't large, just two cells and an anteroom with a desk. No windows either, but it had indoor plumbing.

They locked me in one of the cells, told me they'd bring dinner shortly, and left. I sat on a metal cot covered with a thin mattress and blanket, similar to our beds in the barracks. I was glad for the time alone. I needed to collect my thoughts.

I'd been frightened by our close call, but Mary-Catherine—I have to give her credit—kept a level head and got us out of trouble. I had underestimated her. Or perhaps I had sensed similarities in our behavior. Perhaps in some subtle way her capacity for deceit and cunning was what attracted me in the first place.

Then again, I might have been imagining her so-called talents. The reality was that I had seen an opportunity and taken advantage of it. I couldn't help but smirk as I recalled Stemm's droopy, hangdog face when he saw us emerge from the shed. I had won, and I had behaved the way a good Nazi would, even under duress. In future I could use the girl however I wanted: a spy . . . an ally . . . a whore. I glanced around the walls of my cell. It had been a good day. Now I had to extricate myself from this.

I was still mulling it over when the camp commander, Colonel James, entered the hut accompanied by three men. One, in a US Army uniform, introduced himself in German and said he would be my interpreter. The second, tall, slim, mostly bald, and dressed in civilian clothes, didn't introduce himself. The third was a young American soldier carrying a large pad and pencil. Colonel James was an unremarkable middle-aged man except for a paunch and a carefully groomed handlebar mustache.

"This is an official interview conducted with Reinhard Deschler. Present are myself, FBI Special Agent Pete Lanier, and transcribing the interview is Corporal Sinclair." James paused. "We are doing this in strict adherence with the Geneva Convention protocols."

I focused on the FBI man. Everyone knew about the American crime bureau and their investigative capacity. They were involved in some wartime activities, especially those with criminal intent or espionage within the US. How much did they know about me? Were they going to charge me with rape? Espionage? Under the Führer, those crimes were punishable by death. I had to disabuse them of those notions. I rose from the cot, drew myself up, and folded my arms across my chest.

"If you think this—interview—has any legal standing, you are mistaken," I said. "I will answer only to a German court of law."

The colonel gave me a penetrating look. "Your name, rank, and identification number." The interpreter translated, even though I understood.

I straightened up, puffed out my chest, and spoke clearly. "Reinhard Deschler. SS-Schütze. Assigned to Panzer Division Twenty-One." I clicked my heels and threw out my arm. "Heil Hitler."

The soldier who was transcribing wrote down my words. So did the FBI man. All of them studiously ignored my show of loyalty. Then the colonel cleared his throat.

"Why were you in the shed with the O'Rourke girl?" He homed in right away. The interpreter translated.

"I was responding to her request for help."

"What does that mean?" the colonel asked.

"She had several dozen glass jars to move. She requested that I help her carry them." I paused. "I have done nothing wrong. I don't understand why I am here." I waved an arm around the cell.

The man interpreted what I said accurately. I didn't want them to know how much English I knew. It was one of my only advantages. But when the FBI man stared at me, I could tell he didn't believe me. Americans have no nuance. No subtlety. Their feelings are stupidly plastered across their faces. One wonders how they have managed to rally their forces against us.

The colonel was silent for a moment. "Do you have anything else to say?"

I shook my head.

"You realize we are talking to the girl as well."

I shrugged, as if it was unimportant. As if I didn't care one way or the other. But I knew Mary-Catherine wouldn't break. She had as much to lose as I.

"And you believe she will agree with you?"

I turned the tables on them. "Why shouldn't she? Just what do you suppose did happen?" I folded my arms again.

"There are reports that you and she have"—the colonel raised a hand to his nose and rubbed—"disappeared together several times."

I cocked my head, as if thinking. "She has asked me before to help her move heavy equipment. And I have complied when possible. But, you see, I suffer from vertigo and am occasionally incapacitated. The guards allow me to rest in the back of the truck. Perhaps there is some misunderstanding."

Finally the FBI man spoke up. "Shell shock, is it?" His tone was clearly skeptical.

"A British tank. In the desert with Field Marshal Rommel. In Tunisia." I stared at him. If he wanted to pick a fight, I was ready.

His eyes narrowed. Whether he believed me or not was immaterial. But then he broke eye contact.

Victory.

The men made their exit. I sat on the cot, surprised at how short the interrogation had been. And make no mistake, it *was* an interrogation, not an interview. My dinner was brought in. Although I was famished, I picked at my food. The same team—or perhaps another—was likely on their way to Mary-Catherine. I convinced myself she would not fail me. Hadn't she come up with the deceit in the first place?

I tossed from side to side that night. The truth was I did harbor some doubt. The stakes were high, and her family, because of the boy, was vulnerable. Would she stick to our story? If she didn't, if she blurted out the truth, even inadvertently, I would be incarcerated for the rest of the war. And after.

The next morning, a guard came in and unlocked my cell. "You may return to the barracks."

CHAPTER 16

Wilhelm

"So they believed him?" I asked a guard who spoke German after Deschler was released.

"It would seem."

"Do you?" I asked.

"It's not my place to believe him or not." He shrugged. "Look, I know he's not a popular fellow around here. But they can't go forward without evidence. And from what I hear, there isn't much."

"What are the others saying?"

"That's not your business, Stemm. What I can tell you is that your time at the farm is over. You are all restricted to camp."

"But Mrs. O'Rourke needs us to help with the harvest."

"She's more concerned about her son right now. He has a long recovery ahead."

"And Mary-Catherine—I mean, the elder daughter?"

The guard took out a cigarette, struck a match, and inhaled deeply. "And why would you be asking about her?"

"No reason," I said and trudged back to the barracks.

Kohl was there. "Big day," he said.

Mary-Catherine

Mama stayed at the hospital with Harley for the next few nights. My job was to take the car, pick up Leanne from the neighbors', and feed her supper. The neighbors graciously fed her anyway.

"What happened to Harley, Mary-Catherine?" she said worriedly the next day. "Is he going to be all right?"

I told her an abbreviated version. "He's going to be fine. But it will take a long time."

"Forever?"

I smiled. "Not that long. Maybe Christmas."

She sighed. "But that *is* forever. What's he going to do about school?"

"I don't know. We'll know more tomorrow."

"Can I see him?"

"He's in the hospital, Leanne. And you're not old enough to visit."

She sank back in the front seat and sulked the rest of the way home. I was glad for some silence. I was totally flummoxed. I'd tried to save Reinhard—and myself. Or so I thought. But the guard who saw us emerge from the trees in front of the shed seemed to doubt my story, and Reinhard hadn't said anything one way or the other. In fact, once we came out, he didn't say another word and let them lead him away from me without a backward glance. Of course, I understood why. But still.

I had just put Leanne to bed and come back downstairs when headlights poured through the parlor windows. I ran to the door and watched a military jeep pull up the driveway. A man in uniform climbed out. Even in the dark, I could see the stripes on his jacket. A second man in civilian clothes was with them.

The soldier introduced himself as an MP and gave me his name. The man in civilian clothes stepped in front. "Special Agent Pete Lanier, FBI."

"FBI?" I couldn't conceal my surprise. "What's this about?"

"May we talk?"

"Of course," I said. I hoped my voice didn't sound as fluttery as my stomach felt. I invited them to sit and offered them a glass of water. They declined.

I settled myself on the rocking chair. I knew why they were here. Still, I asked, "How can I help you?"

Lanier, the FBI man, was middle-aged, slim, and as bald as the skin of an orange. "One of the German POWs at Skokie Valley camp is under investigation for something that occurred on your farm. We have some questions."

"My mother isn't here right now. She's at the hospital. My little brother broke his legs."

"Yes. We heard. I'm so sorry," Lanier said. "But it's you we want to talk to. The prisoner's name is Reinhard Deschler."

The soldier took out a pad of paper and a pen.

"Deschler?" I looked away and pretended to think. "I don't think I know who he is."

The men exchanged glances. The soldier scrawled something on his pad. I couldn't tell if they believed me.

Lanier continued. "He claims to have helped you move some jars from a shed to another location."

I gave it another second or two, then nodded. "Oh. Him. I remember now. Yes. He did help me. Yesterday." I let a beat of silence pass. "Why? What's wrong?"

"We have reports that he may have"—Lanier cleared his throat—"acted inappropriately."

I squeezed my lips together. If he was going in for the kill, I would make him say it out loud. "In what way?"

"Did he accost you? Harm you in any way? Make—improper advances?"

I took the high road. "Just what are you insinuating, Agent Lanier?"

There was a long pause. Then: "Did he force himself on you? At any time while he was working on the farm?"

I straightened and folded my arms, gazing from one man to the other. I made myself scowl. "You both need to leave now. Who do you think you are making allegations of this kind? Of course he didn't. I hardly know the man. He is just a laborer. I'm not even sure I'd recognize him in a crowd."

The soldier scribbled on his pad. Lanier leaned back. "I apologize, Miss O'Rourke. I know this is unpleasant, but we had to ask. Did you and he talk while he helped carry the jars? Did he ask you—or in any way request that you help him escape? Or pass him information about the advance of the Allies in Europe?"

I let my mouth fall open. "You're joking."

Lanier didn't reply.

"What would I possibly know about anything like that? I live and work on this farm. The only things I know about the war is what I hear on the radio."

Except for the scratchy sound of the soldier's pen on paper, a stony silence followed.

"You're sure?" Lanier eyed me.

I hoped I sounded indignant. "I'm not sure whether to be angry or happy you're so thorough. Believe me, I know the Germans are our enemy. And just because they are working on my farm does not change that fact. My mother and I are glad for the labor. But that is all."

"Pardon me for saying, but you are an attractive young woman."

I rose from the rocking chair. "I'm not sure what you're implying, Agent Lanier, but I'm going to ask you to leave now. Let me see you out."

We held each other's cold glances for what seemed like forever. Then he pushed up from the sofa, tugged on the lapel of his jacket, and headed out, apologizing again for the intrusion. The MP followed him.

I waited until their jeep had turned out of the driveway before I climbed the stairs. My hands were shaking. Despite my denials, I sensed they didn't believe me. This wasn't over. In fact, it might have been just the beginning. I needed to keep my story straight. I couldn't change a thing.

I got to the top of the steps and started so badly I almost fell back down them. Leanne was crouching at the door to her room. My heart pounded in my chest. How much had she heard?

"What was that all about, Mary-Catherine? Why were those men here?"

"It wasn't important, Leanne."

"But I heard you talking. Did one of the Germans hurt Harley? Is that why he broke his legs?"

Comprehension dawned. Leanne was scared. That was all. I steadied myself and scooped her up in my arms. "No, sweetie. Nothing like that."

"You're sure the Germans aren't going to hurt us?"

I smiled and smoothed the back of her hair. "As sure as I am that the sun's coming up tomorrow, honey. They're absolutely not going to hurt us." Of course that was what she would be worried about. She was a child. All these uniforms. The war. The enemy.

She clung to me as I carried her back into her room. "And Mama's coming home soon?"

"Yes, sweetheart. Tomorrow." I laid her down on her bed. "Hey, how about I read you a story?"

"Okay," she said in a small voice.

Before I'd read two pages, she was asleep. If only everything were that simple.

CHAPTER 17

Wilhelm

The evening was cool for September, so a crowd of us gathered inside the mess tent with cards, chess, and books. The mess had electric lights strung across the ceiling, unlike the barracks, which had no artificial light. Soldiers sprawled on chairs, some at tables, one or two on the floor. Still, a scrim of tension hung over everyone because of Deschler. Most of the men either ignored him or were excessively solicitous.

Deschler, Kohl, and Franz, Deschler's lapdog, were playing a game of skat. I pretended to read a book. The cheerless mood grew oppressive. I went outside, lit a cigarette, and started to walk the perimeter of the camp. We wouldn't be returning to the farm. I wondered if we would spend the rest of the war inside this barbed-wire compound. I wanted to go home to Germany. Or Austria. Even New York. Anywhere but here.

A sudden burst of angry shouts cut into my thoughts. I stopped and cocked my ear.

"Goddammit. You cheated. I saw you!" It was Kohl.

"You're crazy." Deschler.

"I saw you pull that card from under the table. Where did it come from?"

There was a long pause. "You're delusional, Kohl." Deschler again.

Another pause. Then Kohl. "I should have known never to play cards with a Nazi. You don't let the truth get in the way of your plans. Whether it's playing cards or fucking a farm girl. You always have to win, don't you?"

The next thing I heard was the scrape of chairs against the planked floor. I ground out my cigarette and hurried back to the mess tent.

"You're going to regret that, Kohl." Franz's voice now. Loud and belligerent. "You're no better than a dirty Jew."

"And quite possibly a spy," Deschler said coldly. "I saw you whispering with the guard the other night. The one who speaks German."

"What the hell are you talking about?" Kohl shouted.

This was sounding dangerous. I started to jog.

"That was Stemm," Kohl said.

My stomach flipped.

But Deschler ignored Kohl. "You are spying for the Americans, aren't you?" he said. "Don't bother to deny it. You're a traitor to the Reich."

I rushed in. Everyone had stopped what they were doing and crowded around the three men. Kohl, Deschler, and Franz stood around the card table, glaring at one another. All three were stiff with fury. I shouldered my way through, but the number of prisoners slowed me.

Kohl raised his forefinger as if he was aiming a gun and pointed it at Deschler. "You can't even keep it in your pants. You'll fuck anything that moves. An innocent farm girl, a skat player"—he whirled and pointed at Franz—"probably even this sorry excuse for a soldier."

Deschler folded his arms across his chest. His eyes had narrowed to slits. "I've had enough of you, Kohl. I have half a mind to—"

I finally shoved through the crowd and reached them, surprised that no one else had intervened. Where were the level-headed men? The Wehrmacht officers? More important, where were the guards?

"*Achtung!*" I yelled. "Stop! This is not the way German soldiers behave."

"Stay out of this, Stemm," Kohl shouted. "This is not your fight."

"Neither is it yours, Kohl." I turned to Deschler. "Stop this. Tell your man to back off."

The three men didn't respond, but the crowd surrounding us did.

"Go ahead! Kill the SOB!" someone yelled.

"Put the bastard back in the stockade!" someone else cried.

Kohl seemed to soak up renewed energy from the crowd. "Pig. That's what you are, Deschler," he spat out. "A Nazi pig."

Deschler and Franz charged Kohl. Kohl had just enough time to fist his hand, draw back, and belt Deschler on the jaw. Deschler stumbled backward. His hand flew to his cheek. But then Franz landed a fierce blow to Kohl's face. Kohl slammed backward into one of the poles supporting the tent and fell to the floor.

Nothing happened for a moment. I was about to go to Kohl,

when he blinked. Blood trickled from his nose. Slowly, he rolled over and pushed himself up on hands and knees. Franz closed in again, but Kohl stuck out his arm and tripped him. Franz collapsed with a yowl. Kohl slapped him with his right hand full across the face. Franz yelled again. Before Kohl could hit him again, someone else shouted.

"You assholes! You're ruining it for the rest of us!"

"Put them all in a cell!"

And another. "The war is over. You need to learn that."

Kohl, distracted by the crowd, took his attention off Franz for a second. In that second, Franz started to pummel him with his fists. Kohl sagged back against the floor.

Finally, several guards stormed in. "Break it up!" one yelled. He grabbed Franz and muscled his arms behind his back.

"Fun's over!" Another seized Kohl and half carried, half dragged him toward the exit. "All of you," he shouted. "Back to the barracks!"

Curiously, no one grabbed Deschler, who was breathing heavily and favoring his cheek.

Then Colonel James, the camp commander, appeared with a megaphone raised to his lips. "It's over! Back to your barracks. Everyone! On the double." He went to Deschler, slapped a pair of cuffs on his wrists, and led him out of the tent.

CHAPTER 18

Mary-Catherine

An hour after I put Leanne to bed, Mama unexpectedly came home. I'd gone to bed myself, but she must have sensed I was still awake, because I heard her climb the stairs. She came into my room.

"Mary-Catherine...," she said sternly. It was her "I'm not happy with you" voice. "You and I need to talk."

"How's Harley?" I interjected, hoping to delay what I knew was coming.

"In a lot of pain."

"Leanne wants to see him."

Mama didn't reply. Instead she said, "Don't change the subject. I had a visitor at the hospital."

I braced myself. "Who?"

"Colonel James, commander of the POW camp."

The light from the hall spilled into my room. Mama's expression was pinched.

"He told me an interesting story."

I felt suddenly cold.

"According to several prisoners who've been working in the orchard, you have been seen coming out of the shed with a prisoner."

I cleared my throat. "Yes. That's right. He was helping me carry the Mason jars to the pump. So I could wash them before we started canning."

"Apparently, that's not all he was helping you with."

"Mama—"

"Don't," she cut in. "Don't say a word until I'm done." She hesitated. "Do you think you can fool your mother? I know. It's written all over your face."

I searched her eyes. She knew. She really knew.

"I cannot believe you would ruin yourself like this. No one around here is going to want anything to do with you. Or our family. And this—after I expressly forbade you to have anything to do with the prisoners. Not only did you humiliate yourself and the family, but you disobeyed me."

"I—I couldn't help it. If you only knew how I feel. "

Her laugh was harsh. "Really." My stomach clenched. This was a side of my mother I'd never seen.

"Mama, I—"

"No. No explanations." She gazed at me, then shook her head. "The worst part of it is that you have no remorse. You really have no idea what you've done. Giving yourself away like that? Sleeping with a POW. A *German* POW. This is not the type of thing that goes away. You will never live this down. Every time people talk about the camp, they will mention you. Do you know that?"

"I—I think you're wrong."

"Of course you do. You are young."

I decided to keep my mouth shut.

She let out a long breath. "There will be consequences, of course." Her voice became more businesslike. "You will leave the farm immediately."

"But you need me for harvest."

"I changed my mind."

"You need the extra help."

"Not from you."

"But, Mama—"

She cut me off. "Don't argue with me, young lady. I am so very disappointed in you. I trusted you to stay on the farm alone." She turned her head away and began to blink rapidly. "What did I do wrong?" she said softly, as if talking to herself. Then she composed herself. "But you are almost an adult, so you will take responsibility for your conduct."

But I had seen her hesitation. I dove in. "I love him."

She squeezed her eyes shut. Then opened them. I'd never seen my mother look so weary. "And I suppose he told you he loves you too?"

I didn't reply. As if she could read my mind, she let out a long breath. "You are done here, Mary-Catherine. Pack your things. You will be moving to Chicago tomorrow. And you won't be coming back."

CHAPTER 19

Wilhelm

Three days later Colonel James let the men out of the stockade. Kohl came back to the barracks. I looked up from my English-German dictionary. He was pale, and purple bruises limned his eyes. A bandage was taped across his nose. More worrisome, though, was his bearing. Kohl was quiet and reticent, a shadowy version of himself. As if all the fight had gone out of him.

I closed my book and sat up. "What happened in there?"

He didn't answer. Instead he went to his cot and lay down. Then he rolled away from me and curled up in a fetal position.

I went for a walk outside. Usually some of the men played football, or at least kicked the ball around, talking and laughing in small groups. Especially on a crisp sunny day like this. But today it was quiet. No one was outside and anxiety suffused the air.

I slowed my pace. Mary-Catherine, too, had fallen under his spell. I wasn't sure how I felt about her now. That a beautiful young woman could be so easily seduced by a scoundrel like

Deschler was not promising. Then again, she was young and naïve. Perhaps she had just had a bad start. Surely she could begin again, couldn't she?

• • •

I was preoccupied with my thoughts all day, to the point where I had difficulty falling asleep. But I must have dozed off, because I woke abruptly. It was still dark. At first I thought one of the men had a nightmare and was shouting in his sleep. Nightmares were a common ailment. I certainly had my share, when battles, atrocities, and cruelties strafed my dreams, twisting into evil monsters and demons. Tonight, though, no one appeared to be awake. Why was I? Then, amid the men's snores, I heard rustles and muffled footsteps, as if someone was trying to hide their presence.

Instantly alert, I opened my eyes but didn't move. Eventually I made out two shapes that were a little less black than the darkness around us. More often than not, a soldier or two needed to relieve themselves, and the latrine was behind the building, so I didn't pay much attention at first. But the figures didn't go to the latrine. Too late I sensed they had stopped next to Kohl's cot, which was just inside the entrance to the barracks. One of them bent over Kohl, and I heard several sounds. *Thwuck. Thwuck. Thwuck.*

The next moment I will regret for the rest of my life, and I must live with the guilt. The truth is that I was a coward. I knew what was happening. Deschler and Franz were attacking Kohl with what sounded like a knife. I should have stopped it. Sounded an alarm. At least shouted. But I didn't. I lay frozen with fear, sure that if I made even a tiny movement, they would kill me, too. There was no love lost between Deschler and me. He might have decided that, compared to Kohl, I was the lesser of two evils. But that could change at any moment. Especially if I interfered.

It was ironic. I'd never been fearful on the battlefield, even though our mission was to kill or be killed. Killing in war was permissible. But this was murder, which was sinister. Malevolent. So, like a cowering weakling, I kept my mouth shut and pretended to sleep. They covered Kohl with a blanket and turned to leave. After they had passed my cot on their way out, I opened my eyes and watched them slip out the door.

CHAPTER 20

Reinhard

"Hurry!" I whispered to Franz as we raced out of the barracks. He was a few steps behind. "We don't have much time!"

"I'm coming." Franz's breaths came in irregular gasps. I suppose he was grappling with the fact that he'd just killed a man in cold blood. "Wait for me!"

Once they'd let us out of the stockade, I knew what had to be done. I'd taken a long walk around the camp, planning how to do it. The knife was no problem. Franz had won it in a card game, and so far, the guards had not discovered it. And the camp itself was surrounded by thick woods. Plenty of places to hide.

But the compound was bordered by barbed wire atop a chain-link fence, and that had to be fixed. I stared at the fence as I walked, looking for the most unobtrusive spot. I found it behind an empty hut that was used for storage. The next day I "borrowed" a shovel from the truck that drove us back and forth to the farm and stowed it unobtrusively near the hut.

We waited until the middle of the night, stole out of the barracks, and hurried to the hut. I grabbed the shovel and passed it to Franz, who began to dig a hole under the fence. It was a laborious, painstaking process—if we'd had wire cutters, we would have done it much more quickly. At one point the guards made their rounds, and we threw ourselves to the ground, hardly daring to breathe. Fortunately, they must have had a few, because they joked and talked, clearly paying no attention to their surroundings.

Finally, after what seemed like hours, Franz managed to dig a hole that was wide and high enough for me to squeeze through. He stood and admired his handiwork. I snatched the shovel and threw it behind the hut.

"Where is the knife?"

He pulled it out of his back pocket.

"Is it sharp enough?" Franz nodded and ran it across the back of his hand. A few drops of blood popped up.

"*Gut*." And we made our way to Kohl's barracks.

• • •

Now, as I reached the hut afterward, I searched for the hole on the ground. We'd tried to camouflage it, and we'd done such a good job that it took precious seconds to find it. When I did, I let out a relieved breath.

"See if you can lift the piece of fence for me," I ordered. Franz did. I lay on my stomach and began to slither through the hole, using my elbows for purchase. We had trained for this when we were conscripted, so it wasn't difficult. I was almost through when a chorus of shouts erupted. Light exploded, and a siren started to keen.

"*Scheisse!*" Franz hissed. "We're screwed. *Wir haben es verbockt.*"

I wriggled through the remainder of the opening and gestured to Franz. "Come on. Now! *Jetzt!*"

But Franz was burly and much larger than I. He lowered himself to the ground and tried to squeeze through the hole, but it was clear he wouldn't make it. At least not in the few seconds we had left.

"*Nein*," I said. "I must go! I'm sorry."

"*Achtung!*" he yelled. "You must wait!"

"You imbecile!" I hissed. "You just told them where to find us!" I dusted myself off, spun around, and sprinted into the woods alone.

CHAPTER 21

Wilhelm

As soon as Deschler and Franz were gone, I jumped out of bed and hurried to Kohl's cot. I snatched the blanket off and felt for a pulse. Nothing. I tried to shout, but no words came out. I was in one of those nightmares where *der schwarze Mann* is coming after you, but you are frozen with fear. I tried again. Then I went to the middle of the barracks, where a string hung from the lightbulb. I pulled repeatedly, so the light flicked on and off. It was only then that I was able to muster a cry.

"Wake up. Everyone. Kohl—he's dead!"

It took a few minutes for the men to rouse themselves. I threw on some pants, went outside, and yelled for the guards. The two night guards rushed in. I pointed to Kohl. A group of prisoners surrounded his cot.

The guards ran to examine him. "Back. Everybody back. Now!"

The men parted to let the guards through. The first guard glanced at Kohl's body. "Shit!" He spun around and gazed at me, horror unfolding across his face. "What happened? Who did this?" He nodded at the second guard. "Get Colonel James," he ordered. "Right now!"

As the second guard exited the barracks, the prisoners at the other end of the building, who didn't know what was going on, cursed us all for waking them.

The situation seemed to be spiraling out of control when the remaining guard lunged at me, grabbed and wrenched my arms behind my back, and cuffed me. I cried out in pain.

"Stemm, you're coming with me."

"I didn't kill him! I swear it," I spit out. "It was Deschler."

The guard's response was to tighten his grip. "We'll see about that." He shoved me toward the door. As we emerged into the night, the camp's floodlights blazed on, and an earsplitting siren began to wail.

• • •

The night sky was just lightening to gray when we realized, after a thorough search of the camp, that Deschler was gone. Colonel James made the guards drag in Franz, who, without Deschler to pump him up, deflated like a spent balloon. He led them to the hole in the fence.

They threw Franz in the stockade in the cell next to mine.

"Why?" I asked.

He just looked at me.

"Why did you kill him?"

"It was Deschler's idea. We were going to escape. Together. But the son of a bitch double-crossed me."

I raised an eyebrow. "But why? Why did you kill Kohl?"

"Deschler said he was a spy."

"What are you talking about?"

It all spilled out of him then, as if it had been difficult to hold it in. How Deschler thought anyone who wouldn't swear allegiance to Hitler was an enemy, how Deschler was sure there were enemies all over the camp, how he plotted to rid the camp of the worst of them and then escape to join what was left of the German Bund. I listened. What Franz was saying made sense. A sick sort of sense, to be sure. But I myself had heard similar delusions from Deschler's lips. When Franz finished, he looked relieved.

"You told Colonel James?" I asked.

He nodded in sorrow. "I'll never see Deutschland again, will I?"

"No. And you don't deserve to." I shot him a cold glance.

Franz blinked. "Deschler hated you, you know. He thought you were a traitor. But he *knew* Kohl was."

"And now you know that's not true."

Franz squinted as if he wasn't sure whether to believe me. "How would you know?"

"Kohl was just another soldier, Franz. He was my friend. It's Deschler who was the enemy."

Franz blinked again. He kept his mouth shut.

CHAPTER 22

Wilhelm

About an hour later, an armada of men descended on the camp: nearly a dozen Illinois state troopers and two men in civilian clothes, whom I learned were agents from the FBI. One, Special Agent Pete Lanier, was tall, slim, and bald. The other, a young man named Harrison, looked barely older than twenty. The troopers started to search the campgrounds and the surrounding woods again. Colonel James, his translator, and the FBI agents came into the stockade. The commander unlocked my cell.

"You are free to go, Stemm. Sorry for the misunderstanding. Precautions, you know."

The translator repeated his words in German, but I had learned enough English to understand most of what James said. "Yah. Tanks." I shot him a wan smile; there wasn't much to smile about.

"I'd like him to stick around, Colonel," FBI Agent Lanier said, "if it's all right with you."

Colonel James arched his brows and motioned toward the front room of the jail, where there was a small conference table and four chairs. Although it was broad daylight, the window of the room cut into the wall at an odd angle that didn't let in sunlight, and the room was dim.

The guards brought Franz out of his cell and we each took a chair. Lanier interrogated Franz, and he told us everything: Deschler's hatred for soldiers who weren't party members, his suspicion that Kohl was a spy, how they killed him, Deschler's escape. And how he, Franz, had been hoodwinked.

"He never had any intention of allowing me to join him." A trace of sorrow skimmed his face. "He used me."

Lanier let it sink in. Then he nodded. "And now you will be charged with murder in the first degree."

A wave of satisfaction rolled over me; I couldn't help it.

"Prisoner Wendt," Colonel James said. "Do you have any idea where Deschler was headed?"

Franz looked down. "No."

"He never mentioned any plans? Any locations? Any people?" Lanier asked.

"He said I'd find out soon enough."

Lanier folded his arms. "And yet he believed there were spies in the camp. How did he know?"

Franz shrugged. "I'm not sure. But he talked about the Bund a lot."

"Kuhn's outfit? The Bund? It's moribund now." At his pun, a smile tugged at the corner of Lanier's mouth. "And Kuhn is in prison."

"Deschler wanted to revive it. He said the members would spy on the Allies and report back to the Abwehr."

"Tell us. Was he planning to use the farm girl to help him?"

When Franz didn't answer, Lanier added, "You know we had a run-in with Deschler and the girl a while back."

A weary expression from Franz. "Yah."

"What do you know about his relationship with Mary-Catherine O'Rourke?"

Franz hesitated. "He said she might be useful."

I wasn't surprised. I knew Deschler was a bounder. I just didn't know how big.

The troopers interrupted us; they'd finished searching the campgrounds and discovered the shovel.

"This is what you used to dig the hole?" Lanier said.

Franz nodded.

"Where did you find it?"

"Deschler got it off the truck that took him to the farm."

Colonel James's cheeks flamed. "How did he—"

"He hid it under a tarp until he needed it."

The colonel made a note. One of the guards would clearly pay for this negligence. Then Lanier turned to Colonel James.

"Is there anyone here who knows the girl? And Deschler?"

Before the commander could answer, I cleared my throat. "I do."

Lanier stared at me. "Is that so."

I stared back.

"So you were a friend to Deschler?"

"Hardly," I said. "But I was on the same work detail. At the O'Rourkes' orchard."

"So, Prisoner Stemm." Lanier cocked his head. "What do you know about Deschler's—relationship with the girl?"

I told them what I knew. Mary-Catherine playing Frank

Sinatra. Feeding us lunch. The time in the barn when Deschler had vertigo. Their subsequent trips to the shed. Harley's accident.

"And how did you know about the shed?" Lanier asked.

I felt my cheeks get hot. "Everyone knew."

After a beat, Lanier asked Colonel James, "Can you get me a list of the laborers on that farm?"

"Of course." He motioned to one of the guards. "Get it. PDQ."

"This girl must be some dame," Harrison, the young agent with Lanier, cut in. It was the first time he'd said anything since they arrived.

Lanier made a brushing-aside gesture as if his cohort's comment had been gratuitous. Which it had been. "I guess we better find her." He yanked a thumb in my direction. "Why is he in the stockade?"

Colonel James gazed at me.

I answered before he could. "I raised the first alarm."

"But he had nothing to do with the crime?" Lanier asked James.

"Not to my knowledge," the colonel answered.

"But he knows what this Deschler looks like? And the girl?"

The colonel nodded.

Lanier pushed his chair back and stood. "Colonel, let's talk outside. In private."

CHAPTER 23

Wilhelm

Colonel James held a short service for Kohl the next evening. In English, of course. Rather than focusing on the murder, he recited a few lines from the Bible. "Psalm 23 tells us, 'Yea, though I walk through the valley of the shadow of death, I will fear no evil, for thou art with me ...'" Then he read a passage about tolerance from Romans 14. He finished by asking those of us who were comfortable with prayer to say one for Kohl's soul. I found his words comforting; the commander was a good man.

Franz remained in the stockade while officials figured out what to charge him with and whether to hand him over to the FBI or let the army prosecute him. After the service, Colonel James crooked his finger at me.

"Since you know both Deschler and the girl," he went on, "the FBI thinks you can be useful to them."

"How?"

"They want you assigned to them for a few days. A special

mission. They intend to stake out the girl in Chicago and hope that Deschler contacts her. You'll let them know when he shows up. I told them they could have you."

I blinked in surprise. I thought about it. "I will still be a prisoner, yes?"

He nodded. "But the responsibility for your well-being will be transferred to the Bureau for as long as you are with them. You will report to Lanier."

"There is problem," I said in broken English. "If I help, some prisoners—like Deschler—will think I am traitor. I was friend to Kohl. What if there is more like Franz?"

"When this is over, you will be sent to another camp. And"—James paused—"I will recommend you for early release."

I took it all in. Then I said, "Colonel, *danke* for your trust in me." I straightened up, unsure whether to salute him. I didn't. I was leaving the camp.

• • •

First thing the next morning, I packed my duffel. When Lanier saw me, he grimaced.

I froze.

"No, that won't do. You need civilian clothes." He sent his assistant to Colonel James's office. The man returned ten minutes later with shoes, shirt, and American pants. They had a zipper, not buttons. I was unsure how to use it, so Harrison pantomimed what I should do. I managed to zip myself up. Once I was dressed, they looked me over. The shirt was too small, and the pants too big, but a belt kept them from falling. Happily, the shoes were more or less comfortable.

"Perfect," Lanier said. "You look like a hayseed from Wisconsin."

I wasn't sure what he meant, but Harrison laughed.

"Sir." I straightened up and saluted. The American way.

Lanier motioned me to stop. "None of that, Stemm. You're a civilian for the moment."

One of the guards translated.

"*Danke*. Tanks you, sir."

Lanier nodded. "Okay. Let's vamoose."

CHAPTER 24

Wilhelm

Our first stop was the farm. It had been only a week or so since we'd been here, but the orchard was in bad shape. Apples were still hanging from the trees, but they were rotting. The O'Rourkes' harvest was going to be miserable. Lanier and Harrison got out of the sedan's front seat while I climbed out the back.

Mrs. O'Rourke heard us pull up and met us on the front porch. She looked like she had aged ten years, her face pale and haunted. She wiped her hands on her apron and looked at Lanier and Harrison, but when her eyes met mine, she recoiled slightly, as though she recognized me but wasn't sure how.

Lanier introduced himself, Harrison, and then me. Mrs. O'Rourke's eyes widened. "He is from the camp. On our farm detail. Why is he here?"

"He knows your daughter, Mrs. O'Rourke. And, more

importantly, Reinhard Deschler. Colonel James has deputized him to work with us to recapture the man."

She sniffed in disdain. "You can't tell me you trust him? He's a German."

"He's a model prisoner. The commandant of the camp trusts him."

She pursed her lips, still wary. "And what will you do if you find him? Deschler?"

"He will face charges of murder and escape from custody. He will be in prison for the rest of his life."

She raised her thumb to her mouth and bit it.

"We just wanted to confirm that your daughter is now working at Republic Steel, correct?"

Mrs. O'Rourke nodded. "After what happened, I had to—"

"No need to explain, Mrs. O'Rourke. Where is she living?"

"At a rooming house for young women working at the mill. Torrence Avenue, I believe. Wait."

She went inside and returned a moment later with a scrap of paper on which an address was printed in pencil. "Good luck, Agent Lanier," she said.

He nodded and we made our way back to the automobile.

She called out as we were climbing back in. "You—you don't think she's in danger, do you?"

Lanier raised a hand in farewell. "We'll do our best to see she's not."

CHAPTER 25

Mary-Catherine

Working in a steel plant can break your spirit as well as your back. It's an inferno inside, especially if your job is to move giant containers of molten iron or pour red-hot ingots just out of the blast furnace. During the first few days, I was exhausted, homesick, and depressed. I wanted to be anywhere except Republic Steel—even back on the farm, where a cooling breeze might waft across the fields. Gradually, though, I got used to it.

The entire plant was devoted to the war effort. I was taught to be a welder. I wore baggy pants and goggles; my hair was tied back with a kerchief, and I wore a soft hat on top. Thick leather gloves protected my hands from the acetylene torch. Some days I beveled armor plates; on others I was a scraper, which meant smoothing loose surface imperfections with my torch to get the plates ready for welding. On those days I wore a helmet, which we were expected to buy. A lot of the girls stenciled their names across the top. We were allowed two ten-minute breaks plus twenty minutes for lunch. My only consolation was the brisk October air, which we soaked up like bees do honey.

More than half of the employees were women. But they were friendly, and I soon got in with some gals from Indiana, Ohio, and Michigan, who were boarding at the same house as I. Most of us were on the morning shift, which meant we were done by two in the afternoon. We'd clean up and eat supper together on the first floor, but the rest of the day was our own. I was one of the youngest—many were mothers with children, and they passed around lots of baby pictures. When they asked why I—not yet twenty—was there, I said my mother on the farm needed money while my father was fighting the Japs. I also talked up Harley. He had polio, I fibbed, and needed an iron lung. They accepted me without question.

We usually spent the evenings at the tavern a few blocks away on 111th Street. It was a shabby place, with a bar so old that the rings from generations of glasses had become practically invisible. I developed a taste for beer, cigarettes, and bawdy jokes. After a few evenings, I couldn't think of a time I'd ever had so much fun.

Of course, Reinhard was never far from my thoughts. On the crisp October evenings when we walked home from the bar, I wondered how he was doing at the camp. Our daily lives weren't so different. We were both prisoners, forced to do grueling work under strict supervision. I wondered if—and how—I would ever see him again.

Even if I didn't, I tried to convince myself I had no regrets. I had given myself to him willingly. Not the awkward fumbling Steve and I had shared in high school. I had come into my own as a woman. I listened to my new friends discussing their husbands and lovers. They were mature women who knew how to satisfy and be satisfied in return. I decided I was too.

CHAPTER 26

Mary-Catherine

Two weeks later, I was walking back from the tavern, arm in arm with my new friend, Pauline, counting the cracks in the sidewalk, when I smelled the odor of an unwashed body. Pauline wrinkled her nose as well, just as a man stepped out of the shadows. We froze. As the streetlight caught him, I saw he was disheveled. He wore baggy pants and a shirt, both of which looked filthy, and he needed a shave. And yet there was something familiar about him.

"Mary-Catherine?"

I took a closer look. There were the piercing blue eyes. The blond, albeit matted hair. I staggered back. Goose bumps rose on my arms. "Reinhard?"

He nodded but scowled at Pauline. I glanced over. She was staring wide-eyed. As if she was staring at a monster from the depths of the ocean. I placed my hand on her arm. "It's all right, Pauline. I'll catch up with you back at the house."

Her eyes narrowed. "Are you sure, kiddo?"

I nodded.

She hesitated. I knew she was uncertain whether to leave me alone with him.

"It's all right," I said bravely. I had my doubts, but I knew he wouldn't talk if she was around.

Once she was out of sight, I stepped closer. He smelled rancid: body odor, manure, and worse. I decided it didn't matter and planted him with kisses. "How did you get here? When? How were you able to get out of camp? I'm so happy!"

He grabbed my shoulders and pushed me away. "I escaped."

My jaw dropped. I stiffened. "You escaped? How? Why?"

He hesitated just a beat. "For you, my love. I did it for you."

For the second time that evening, my mouth opened. "I don't know what to say."

"I told you we would be together, no?"

I nodded slowly. "But—how? How did you do it?"

"I'll tell you when we have time. Actually, it seems I can be useful. I am to meet some men."

"What men?"

"It—it's classified. But I need your help."

"Classified? What does that mean? Did these men help you escape?"

"No." He smiled. "We will be running some operations soon. But I will need to find them. Will you help? They are somewhere in Chicago."

I nodded again, but my mind was on other things. I ran my hand down his cheek. "Of course I'll help you, my love." I smiled back. "How on earth did you find me?"

"You told me where you worked. I followed you home. And then"—he yanked a thumb—"to the bar."

"Because you couldn't stay away?" I murmured. "You had to see me?"

Another beat of silence. Then he pasted on a wan smile. "Yah. That is it."

"Where will you live?"

"With you. Like we planned."

I shook my head. "That's not possible. The rooming house is for women only."

"So you will move out. We will find a place together."

"Reinhard, I don't have the money for that. Do you?"

"Not yet." He pressed his lips together. "I need a place to stay for a few nights."

"Let me think," I said. A moment later I brightened. "I know. There's an abandoned house a few blocks from here. We pass it on our way to the plant. People use it to squat."

"To what?"

"It means staying in a place you don't own. It's not far. You can stay there tonight. But . . ." It was beginning to dawn on me that his presence here in Chicago could be a problem.

He picked up on my doubt. "Yes. But what am I to do tomorrow? I need—I want to be with you."

I ran a hand through my hair. "Well . . . I guess I could be sick tomorrow morning. The girls have the day shift, and Mrs. Bosworth does her marketing around nine. If you come to the house then, at the very least you can take a shower and we can . . ." I grinned.

"Yah." His voice was flat.

I ignored it. "Oh, Reinhard, I can hardly believe it. You came. You're here. You really do love me."

Again a tiny smile. "Where is this house?" he asked.

"Come." I tucked his hand under my arm and led him down the street. "I can't wait to hear how you escaped, how you got to Chicago. Everything." Then I stopped. "Wait a sec." I dropped his hand. "Won't they be looking for you? Do you think it's safe for you to be here? I mean, they know you and I—um—are involved."

"That is why I need to disappear. No one will find me—us—in downtown Chicago."

I frowned. "I'm not so sure. You know a G-man came to see me."

"What is this 'G-man'?"

"The FBI. Everyone says they're awfully good at getting their man."

"I cannot worry about them. I need to sleep."

"All right." I started forward again. "We'll talk about it tomorrow."

He shot furtive glances in both directions, then followed.

CHAPTER 27

_____

Reinhard

It was clear that the house off Torrence Avenue, a ramshackle building, had not been occupied for a while. The door was partially open, and the windows were boarded up. Even in the dim streetlight, I saw that the lawn was overgrown with weeds. As we entered, a horrid sour smell of dirty clothes and unwashed bodies wafted over us, but there didn't appear to be anyone "squatting," as Mary-Catherine had explained. She left soon afterward. I did not blame her.

I checked the house to make sure I was alone. A tattered blanket lay in an upstairs room. It, too, stank, of body odor and urine, but it was the only covering I could find, and the night was chilly. I brought it downstairs and spread it on top of a threadbare carpet. It did nothing to warm me. I considered turning on the stove in the kitchen but worried I might set the house on fire.

It had been a punishing few days. Once I was free of the camp, my first task was to swap my prison garb for civilian clothes. I broke into a house near the camp, which was fortunately empty, and stole some men's clothing. Then I hiked five miles to the train station in town. In the camp we could hear the clacks and hisses of the trains at night as they rolled through. But no trains were running at the moment, and I worried I would have to hide until darkness fell again the next day. Finally, though, just before dawn, a freight train rumbled down the tracks heading for Chicago. Some of its cars had sliding doors.

I'd never hopped a train before, but I'd heard stories of desperate Jews and Communists who'd fled the SS by climbing aboard a moving train. Americans did as well, during their economic depression, but it was a dangerous activity. Still, I had no other option. I could not ask for a ride from a truck driver—he would hear my heavy German accent. I had no money to buy a ticket, and it was too far to walk. I hid behind the station house and waited.

The train slowed to a crawl as it slid into the station. Before I lost my courage, I hoisted myself up between two cars and grabbed the edge of one. It was made of serrated metal, and if I prized my fingers just so, I could hang on. My feet were another matter. They were planted on top of the coupler between the cars, but the steel contraption had been designed to be flexible, and it was in constant motion. I was in a highly precarious situation. A sudden stop or acceleration would cause me to lose my balance, and I would be thrown under the train to undoubtedly suffer a gruesome death.

I had to get inside one of the cars. The train did not stop at the station, but thankfully, a short distance past, it slowed even more, and I was able to jump down, pry open one of sliding doors, and hoist myself inside. But just as I was closing the door, congratulating myself on my achievement, a powerful stench sent a jolt of revulsion through me. I spun around.

I was in a car crowded with cattle, presumably on their way to the stockyards. The stink of manure was nauseating. Further, my sudden presence had disturbed them and they were snuffling, mooing, and stamping their feet. I wedged myself into a corner, afraid they would somehow manage to stomp me to death. I crouched, trying to make myself less of a target, at the same time trying not to slip in the muck of manure and waste.

It was then that the absurdity of my situation struck me. Why was I—a loyal soldier of the Reich—crammed among a herd of filthy, bleating cows? How had I ended up hungry, tired, and dirty, with no place to stay? I was no better than a tramp or an outlaw. An overwhelming sense of failure washed over me. Perhaps I should abandon my plans. Surrender, as Rommel did in North Africa.

I was mulling it over when a memory from my childhood surfaced, something I'd not recalled until now, so deeply had it been buried. My father had been a volatile man; he was usually angry, especially toward my mother. He berated and criticized her continually. She was no better than a peasant, a second-class citizen, even a whore. She did not deserve a man like him. One day he struck her across the face. She staggered back, a bright red welt rising on her cheek. Tears rimmed her eyes. Then he struck her again. I was only four or five, and I hurried over to comfort her, but my father held me back. He said there was no excuse for my mother's wretched behavior . . . her inability to cook or clean . . . her failure as a wife and mother. She was pathetic, my father yelled.

"Let this be an example for you, Reinhard. You must always be strong. Do you hear me? You must never cry. Or let anyone defeat you. Do you understand?"

I nodded. As I matured, I came to regard my mother with pity, even superiority. And when she hanged herself the day after I turned twelve, I agreed with my father that it was because she was weak.

CHAPTER 28

Reinhard

I do not recall falling asleep but I suddenly woke, disoriented. It took a moment to remember I was in a house in Chicago that squatters used. Daylight peeked through the edges of boarded-up windows. I got up and peered through a gap. A thick overcast threatened rain. What time was it? Had I overslept and missed the meeting with Mary-Catherine? I hadn't slept at all two nights ago and only sporadically last night.

I wondered how to wash up—the house had no running water—when I heard a soft shuffling. Steps on the ceiling above. Footsteps. That was what woke me. I was no longer alone!

Panic skimmed my nerves. Who was here? How had he entered the house? I thought I had locked what remained of the door. I quietly searched the first floor. No one. Which meant whoever was above me had seen me on his way upstairs. He could have hurt me. Even killed me. But he hadn't. He hadn't even woken me up. All the same, I should find out who this person was and eliminate the threat. I rubbed my face.

Then I stopped, embarrassed at my own stupidity. I had no weapons except my fists. What if the man upstairs was—what did Mary-Catherine call them?—a G-man. Then again, if he was, wouldn't he have arrested me, or worse, by now? What if he was a hobo who planned to rob me? He would have done so already. Of course, I had nothing of value to steal.

Still, I was in unfamiliar territory. An alien land and culture. Oh yes, I could bluster my way through the days, appearing superior to everyone. But that was the only way I knew to get along with my father. To escape the beatings, which multiplied after my mother was gone. His volatile nature taught me how to plant fear in my enemies before they did the same to me. However, this was different. I was alone and defenseless in a strange country. I gulped down air.

I recalled a saying that it is when one is most afraid and yet does something bold that one is truly courageous. I swallowed, my Adam's apple nearly choking me. I crept to the steps and listened. The noise upstairs had stopped. Cautiously, carefully, I climbed up. A step squeaked. I froze. Nothing happened. I mounted another step. Another creak. Still no one appeared.

When I finally reached the landing, I saw light seeping under the door of the room from which I'd taken the blanket the previous night. I tiptoed toward it. The door was slightly ajar. I peeked in.

A man with coal-black skin and nubby hair peered back at me. A candle flickered on a crate beside him. I stumbled back. I had not seen many black men before. Naturally, I knew of Jesse Owens from the Berlin Olympics, but only through photographs and newsreels. But *Schwarzes* were rare in Deutschland, and there were none at the camp or in farm country. I had seen brown-skinned men from time to time in North Africa, but always from a distance. This man looked like a giant, with thick arms and a barrel chest. He smelled different, his scent overlaid with a strange earthy odor that hinted at musk. Rich and fertile in its own way.

He reached into his pocket. Was he fishing out a gun? I backed out and clattered furiously down the steps. I had reached the first floor and was on my way out when I heard a few chords of music. It sounded tinny and wobbly, but it was music. A harmonica. A moment later the music stopped but a clear baritone sang out.

"Swing low, sweet chariot, comin' for to carry me home . . ."

I had never heard a song like this before. It was a simple tune, and yet it was haunting. When he finished singing, he started with the harmonica again. Then he stopped and called out. "Come on up, man. I ain't gonna hurt ya."

Something in his tone told me he wasn't a threat. I climbed back upstairs. He played another tune I didn't know. I hesitated at the door. His eyes were so bloodshot that the whites blazed in comparison. Clothed in little more than rags, he grinned as he played. I wondered how he was able to smile and blow at the same time.

When he finished the second tune, he said. "You a squatter too?"

I didn't know what to say, so I nodded. I wondered what he had done to become homeless. Was he running, too?

"Yeah, well, I figured. Thought I mighta seen you down at the railroad station yesterday."

I was at a loss for words. I didn't want to talk; he'd pick up my heavy accent. I swallowed again.

"But chu gotta give me back my blanket. Only thing I got in this world."

I opened my mouth but caught myself in time. I went downstairs, retrieved the blanket, and tossed it to him when I returned.

"Thank ye kindly," he said, then blew into the harmonica again.

I pointed to the place on my arm where a wristwatch would sit.

The man stopped his music. "I got all the time in the world, man."

I flipped up my hands and pointed again.

"What? The cat got your tongue?" He waited for me to reply, but when I didn't he shrugged. "Ain't got no idea. It's early. I jes' got back from the bar not too long ago." He stifled a huge yawn.

I turned away and went into what was left of the bathroom to relieve myself. I stole a look in the mirror on the wall over the sink. Deep circles ringed my eyes, my face was dirty and pale, and my lips were cracked. Fear was etched across my face. I finger-combed my hair, dreaming what I would give for a bucket of water. That reminded me of Mary-Catherine, and how she'd brought me exactly that during my bout of vertigo back at the farm. She was a sweet girl. With a sudden jolt of clarity, I realized I wanted to see her.

CHAPTER 29

Mary-Catherine

I told the girls I wasn't feeling well the next morning. Pauline, who'd been with me when Reinhard appeared the night before, cocked her head and shot me a quizzical look but didn't say anything. I stayed in bed until all the girls had gone and Mrs. Bosworth went out to market. Then I jumped up, took a quick bath, and styled my hair. I crept downstairs to see if Mrs. Bosworth had come back unexpectedly. She hadn't, so I made a new pot of coffee and poured a cup.

A few minutes later there was a tentative knock on the back door off the kitchen. I hurried over and opened it.

Reinhard.

He smiled when he saw me and swept me into his arms. I would have been thrilled had the smell on him not been so repulsive. I scrunched up my nose and pushed him away. "You stink."

An unhappy expression spread across his face. "I have not had the chance to bathe."

"Well, you will now." I led him upstairs. "You have to be quick. Mrs. Bosworth could be coming home anytime."

I filled the tub with water. It wasn't as hot as I would have liked, but hot water was scarce with so many girls bathing every day. I tossed him a towel and told him to give me his clothes.

"But they are the only ones I have."

"Let me see if I can wash them. Mrs. Bosworth's husband was KIA in the Pacific—that's why she opened her home to us gals—but she still has his things. I'll grab what I can. Then, after I wash yours, I'll put them back. If we're lucky, she'll never know."

He flashed me a grateful smile, closed the bathroom door, and a moment later, tossed out his foul-smelling clothes. I threw them into a corner; I would wash them later. I snuck down to Mrs. Bosworth's bedroom. Sure enough, I found a pair of her husband's pants and a shirt. Even an undershirt, socks, and shoes. This was my lucky day.

As I came back up with the clothes under my arm, Reinhard came out of the bathroom with the towel wrapped around his waist. I'd never seen his body in broad daylight; our encounters had been in the dimly lit shed. I gently unwrapped the towel and took a moment to admire him. His body was lean and sinewy, and his skin was so pale it reminded me of the white hydrangeas in the garden. And, of course, there were his blue eyes and sandy hair. I smiled.

He colored and returned what I took to be a self-conscious smile. "It is all right?"

"It's perfect." I took his hand and led him into my room.

"What about the woman? Mrs.—"

"Bosworth? It will be okay," I said. He usually was fast, anyway. This time, though, he went slowly. He ran his hands all over my body in a soft, almost tender way. Then he closed his eyes, kissed me deeply, and trailed his lips where his hands had been. He'd never done that before, and I was so excited that for the first time, I climaxed before him.

• • •

When we both came up for air, I whispered, "What's come over you?"

He ran his hand down my cheek. "I missed you so much, Mary-Catherine. I—I—"

Suddenly the front door opened, and a woman's voice called out. "Mary-Catherine? How are you feeling, dear? Should I make you a cup of tea?"

We both froze. "Crap!" I whispered. "She's back!"

Reinhard whispered back, horrified. "I cannot be caught. I must not."

I nodded. "Get under the bed. Now."

He rolled off me, still as naked as a jaybird, and slid under the mattress. I scrambled under the covers and pulled them up to my chin.

"Are you asleep?" Mrs. Bosworth said. I heard her tread on the stairs. Then I remembered his clothes, which I'd thrown into the corner. Shit. It was too dangerous for her to come into the room. I jumped out of bed and called out.

"I'm awake, and I'm feeling much better, Mrs. Bosworth. Hold on while I put on a housecoat."

I grabbed my robe, threw it on, and opened my door. Just as I was exiting, I saw the towel Reinhard had used crumpled on the floor of the hall, where I'd tossed it after I took it off him. I grabbed that, too, and wound it around my head. As she reached the top of the stairs, I closed the door to my room. She peered into the bathroom, where a tiny bit of steam still clung to the mirror.

"Oh, I see you took a bath," she said.

"I—I thought it would make me feel better," I replied. "And it did," I added hastily.

"Well, that's just fine, Mary-Catherine. Let me make you a cup of tea."

"Um, I already had coffee. In fact, I made a new pot. I hope you don't mind." I didn't say that I'd planned to share it with Reinhard. He must be starving.

"Of course I don't mind." She started to go downstairs.

"I'll just get dressed, ma'am; then I'll help you with the groceries."

"Well, thank you, dear."

We exchanged smiles, and I watched her descend the stairs slowly, one at a time. She wasn't old, but she was starting to behave more tentatively, as if her body had become more fragile. Not that climbing downstairs was much of a challenge. I hurried back into my room, bent down, and whispered to Reinhard.

"I don't know how to get you out. You'll have to wait."

"Hurry," his muffled voice replied.

"Get dressed. I'll be back up as soon as I can."

He slid out and dressed. I bit my lip. We were in a fix, and I was scared. I had just pulled on my trousers and a shirt when Mrs. Bosworth called up.

"Mary-Catherine, I have to go back to the market. I forgot to take my ration card and we're very low on sugar."

I sucked in a breath. Aloud, I said, "Oh, okay. While you're gone, I'll put away the other things."

"That would be wonderful." The front door closed with a thump.

I grinned at Reinhard and threw my arms around him. "Saved by a sweet tooth!"

CHAPTER 30

Reinhard

When I came down the steps, dressed in the clothes of Mrs. Bosworth's dead husband, Mary-Catherine slapped together a sandwich and threw some fruit, cheese, and bread into a paper bag. "I know you're starving, but you have to leave. Here's something to tide you over."

"But where shall I go?"

"Where did you plan to go when you escaped?"

"To find you." It was true.

"So now you have. But surely you had other ideas. A backup plan, at least."

I hesitated. Then, "I can still be of use to the Reich."

She stiffened. "What did you say?"

"I want to gather intelligence about your countrymen and what they are doing. Especially with the atomic bomb. We know they are working on it."

A stricken expression came over her. "You want to spy on us?"

I didn't answer.

"Reinhard, you can't do that. It's—impossible!"

"Mary-Catherine, I have always been loyal to my homeland. You know that."

"But Germany is our enemy. America's enemy."

"Most Americans have German blood in their families."

"So what? That doesn't make Hitler right."

I ran my tongue around my lips. What had I expected? I should have known she would react badly. I should try a different approach. I needed her.

I smiled. "We love each other. At least I love you. And you know I'm a German soldier."

"Yes, but—" She pressed her lips together and furrowed her brow. I couldn't tell what she was thinking. I went on.

"We have had—well, we have had relations. The most intimate thing lovers can do."

She kept her mouth shut.

"You've already shown me that our love is more important to you than the war." I paused. "And I feel the same way. But I have an opportunity now, and I do not want to squander it. I am not asking you to get involved. You should continue to work at the mill. After all, we will need money."

A long silence ensued. Then, "Reinhard, I don't make much. And I send anything that's left over home." She started to pace. "I just don't know. This is not the way I pictured things would go."

Did that mean she had yielded? I let the silence hang a bit longer. Then, as if I had just thought of it, I said, "All right. I will get a job."

I waited for her to agree. And to soften into the amenable, sweet Mary-Catherine I knew.

But her voice was sharp. "Doing what? Who's going to hire a Kraut?"

I winced.

"Especially one who escaped from a camp."

I scrambled for a response. "They do not need to know that. And there are like-minded people here. Your Bund was quite active, yah?"

"It's over now. And Fritz Kuhn is in jail."

"Still, as I said, there are Americans who have a 'special' attachment to Germany. I will find them."

"You're asking me to commit treason. Or, at the very least, ignore yours."

"I'm not asking you to do anything. Except love me." I held out my arms. "You do, yah?"

She came into them. "Yes." Her voice was small.

"Then it is all right." I kissed her tenderly.

Afterward, she backed away and threw me an odd look. We both knew it wasn't. But there was no time to discuss it. Mrs. Bosworth could return at any moment.

"Mary-Catherine, can you spare a dollar? I will pay you back. I promise."

"I already told you. I haven't got any."

"I'm desperate."

Mary-Catherine

I was flummoxed. I needed a long sit, as Mama used to call them, where we convened at the kitchen table with coffee or tea and solved our knotty problems. A wave of homesickness washed over me. I missed my mother. She would know what to do.

But there wasn't time. Tension sliced through me, curdling my stomach. I could only imagine how Reinhard felt. I continued to pace. As I did, the seed of a solution presented itself. Unfortunately, it was a bad one.

Except we were in a jam. And I had only a minute or two to decide what to do. It was suddenly hard to breathe; I was close to panic. I hated myself for what I was thinking, but it wouldn't go away.

My friend Pauline was engaged. Her young man, stationed in Bakersfield, California, was due to ship out anytime now. Before he'd been drafted, he scraped together enough money for an engagement ring. It was modest, but it was real gold set around a tiny emerald. She showed it to me one day when she was afraid he might not make it home. She usually kept it hidden in one of her shoes because of its value. She made me promise not to tell anyone it was there.

Now, though, I thought about that ring. I liked Pauline. She was a sweet girl. We had befriended each other when we were both in vulnerable states. If I did what I was thinking, I would never be able to look her in the eye again. Then I looked over at Reinhard. Even if he was telling the truth—that he'd escaped only to be with me—which I wasn't sure was the case, what I was thinking was wrong.

But he loved me. He'd broken out of a POW camp just to find me. And I loved him. Wasn't I supposed to do whatever I could for the man I loved?

"Mary-Catherine. Please." He was begging now.

I didn't know what to do. Why couldn't I mull it over? If I decided to do it, I could give it to him in a day or two.

Instead, I trudged upstairs. Some of the girls locked their doors when they weren't there. Pauline didn't. She figured if she kept it unlocked no one would think she had anything valuable. I opened her door slowly and went to the armoire that served as her closet. I opened the door, bent down, and spotted her shiny black pumps. I felt inside the left shoe and found the ring right away. It was wrapped in tissue paper. I squeezed my eyes shut. Then I took it out of the shoe, stood, and walked out of her room. I crossed the hall and went back downstairs. I couldn't pretend I didn't know what I was doing. I knew all too well.

Without a word, I handed the parcel to Reinhard. His eyes widened when he unwrapped it and saw what it was. He pulled me to him and kissed me. Then he slid the ring into his pocket, opened the back door, and was gone.

CHAPTER 31

Wilhelm

Three of us left for Chicago at dawn the next morning: Lanier, the FBI man; an army intelligence officer who spoke German; and me. We piled into a black Ford sedan. They made me sit in the back with the army man, but they didn't cuff me. All of us were in civilian clothes.

I'd visited Berlin twice; Frankfurt, too. But Chicago was altogether different. It was huge. Lanier told me the city stretched twenty-five miles, or more than forty kilometers, from south to north. And that was just the city proper. The surrounding areas added to its size. It made Frankfurt, and even Berlin, look like a country village.

We drove south on a twisty wooded road called Sheridan for several miles. It offered glimpses of Lake Michigan on one side. Then we turned onto a boulevard called Lake Shore Drive and I could see the lake clearly. The entire city hugs the lake, and they say it's impossible to get lost since the water is always east. The lake itself is more like an ocean, with high waves and dangerous storms. Both Lanier and the army captain, a beefy man named George Cranston, told me of the shipwrecks, and even a warplane or two, that had been swallowed up by the water.

But it was the skyline, which I saw at first from a distance, that took my breath away. Tall buildings with graceful spires swept up to the sky. Nestled between them were other structures, not as high, but all of them sturdy and elegant. As we got closer, I could see that some were crowned with graceful arches, while others had decorative gargoyles. And everything was new and modern. As a former architecture student, I was overwhelmed. Not even Berlin, with its stately but stodgy landmarks, could match the raw power and beauty of this city.

We jogged west and then south again on Field Boulevard, passing the museum, whose columns bore a slight resemblance to our Brandenburg Gate. Then past the Museum of Science and Industry, just ten years old, the vision of a wealthy American Jew who modeled it after our Deutsches Museum in Munich.

Eventually we arrived at Republic Steel in the southeast part of the city. We were farther away from the lake, and it seemed hotter here. Apparently the morning shift was over, and workers, both men and women, swung through the gates. Most wore hard hats and carried metal lunch pails. I noticed three main buildings, all just one story high, sprawled behind a chain-link fence. Tall smokestacks belched black smoke, and the odor of smelting floated through the air. Next to the buildings inside the fence were railroad tracks, and several flatbed cars stood at the ready. The contrast between the beauty of downtown Chicago and the ugliness of this facility was disheartening. It was hard to believe they were both part of the same city.

Cranston stayed in the car with me while Lanier climbed out and went through what looked like the main gate. He returned about ten minutes later. Alone. He looked thoughtful.

"Well?" Cranston asked.

"She didn't come in today. A girl she lives with said she was sick."

Lanier and Cranston exchanged glances. They didn't say anything, but the tension in the car deepened. Lanier drove to a residential street about a kilometer, I guessed, from the plant. We parked in front of a comfortable-looking clapboard house with three stories. A small garden in front had been tended over the summer, but its stalks and stems were bare now.

"This should be the place," Lanier said. He squinted at a slip of paper he pulled out of his pocket.

"You want to cuff him?" Cranston yanked a thumb in my direction.

Lanier twisted around. He looked me up and down. "Do I have to worry about you?"

I cocked my head.

"You're not gonna give me any trouble in there, right?"

I shook my head. "No trouble."

"I think we'll be okay." He turned back and let out a sigh, as if he was bone weary. Then he slid out of the car. We followed.

CHAPTER 32

_____

Mary-Catherine

I was in my room trying to read when the doorbell rang. It was around shift-change time in the factory, so I figured one of the gals had lost her key. I was surprised when Mrs. Bosworth called upstairs.

"Mary-Catherine, there are some gentlemen to see you."

Gentle*men*. Not gentle*man*. I frowned. Who would be visiting me? In the middle of the day? Reinhard had just left, and I wasn't expecting to see him for a day or two. "Coming."

I clattered down the stairs but stopped short when I saw who it was: the FBI agent who had interviewed me two weeks ago. With two men. I studied the other men and stiffened. One of the two was a POW from the camp. Wilhelm, I thought his name was. My pulse started to race. "What are *you* doing here? How did—"

The FBI man cut me off. "Special assignment." He watched me carefully.

A queasy feeling spread through my gut. "Why are you here?" I tried to sound earnest.

Lanier told me about Reinhard's escape.

I pressed my hand against my chest. "Oh, that's dreadful!" Lanier didn't react. "You must be going crazy." I hesitated. "Is that why you're here?"

"Have you heard from him? Seen him? Had any communication from him over the past two days? A letter? A note? A phone call?"

I pressed my lips together. "No. In fact, I hardly know the man. And I haven't seen him since he worked on the farm."

"Is that so." Lanier inclined his head and gazed at me. It wasn't a question.

As I recalled, he'd done the same thing when he first came to the house. My heart banged in my chest so urgently I was sure they could hear it. "Yes."

No one spoke for a long moment. Then Lanier scribbled something on a small notepad, tore off the paper, and handed it to me. "Well, if you do hear from him, we want you to call this number as soon as possible. And if I were you, I wouldn't talk to him. He's a dangerous man."

"Dangerous?"

"Didn't your mother tell you?"

I shook my head.

"He killed another prisoner."

I gasped. "What?"

"Someone who didn't agree with his Nazi politics. He and another inmate stabbed the man in cold blood."

"No!" Suddenly I felt cold. I folded my arms on my chest to keep from shivering.

"Why do you say 'no'?"

"I—I just can't believe it! I mean, that—that sort of thing isn't supposed to happen here. Maybe in Europe..." I was babbling now, not understanding my own words. My voice trailed off.

Lanier's eyes narrowed. "Miss O'Rourke, Deschler is an ardent supporter of Hitler. He's proved that on many occasions. He's no dummy. He knows how to manipulate people to get his way." He paused as if to let his words sink in. "When you add in his utter disregard for human life, that makes him dangerous as well as desperate. He is probably armed by now and hiding somewhere in Chicago."

I swallowed. The FBI agent clearly suspected I knew more than I was saying. I had to get them out of here. Or if I couldn't, at least change the subject. I glanced over at the German soldier. Wilhelm. He, too, was watching me. "I still don't understand. Why is *he* here?"

"He can identify Deschler."

This was not good. How much did this prisoner know? Had Reinhard said something to him about us? My insides started to melt, and I struggled to keep my composure.

"So you'll call us if you see him? Or hear from him?"

I nodded. "Of course, Agent Lanier."

CHAPTER 33

___

Wilhelm

As we trudged back to the car, I could see from the men's expressions that they didn't believe Mary-Catherine. I didn't either, and when we climbed inside the car, I told them so.

"Why, Stemm?" Lanier asked.

I told them how Mary-Catherine had pumped me when Deschler, ill from his vertigo, didn't come with the rest of us to the farm. I told them how I'd seen him in the barn with Mary-Catherine, as well as coming out of the shed together the day Harley broke his leg. How Deschler had shot me a look of triumph despite being thrown into the stockade.

"What exactly did she say when she asked about him?"

I summarized our conversation: how we'd tried to overcome the language barrier; how I'd told her Deschler would be back the following day; how a wide grin came across her face when she understood.

"That's good, Stemm. Very good." Lanier rubbed his hands together. "We knew she was lying, but this helps build our case."

I nodded. My infatuation with her was gone. Although she was beautiful, she was almost as callous and deceitful as Deschler. Even so, I think she was shocked when we told her Deschler had killed Kohl. There had been a determined, calculating frown on her face, as if she was sifting the events of the summer, fitting together the pieces of a puzzle. Perhaps murder was a bar too high even for her.

We spent the next two days tailing Mary-Catherine and staking out the rooming house. We knew Deschler wouldn't come in daylight, but Lanier and Cranston wanted to be sure he wasn't leaving a message for her in some out-of-the-way dead drop.

Sometimes Lanier was with me, sometimes Cranston. In the evening, they both appeared. They brought me coffee and food, allowed me to take breaks, and were unfailingly polite. Although I didn't get everything they said, I understood the gist of it. They mulled over whether he would be indicted for treason, in addition to murder and escape. Each man presented what seemed to be persuasive arguments. But I didn't much care about the politics. In a strange way I hoped Reinhard wouldn't show up. I feared the confrontation that would ensue.

Being so close to Mary-Catherine throughout the day and night reinforced my opinion of her. She was assigned to the early shift and left the house before six, usually with a group of other young women. They wore trousers, something German women would never do. They carried metal hats as well as lunch pails. They laughed and joked, each trying to outdo the others with their stories. Mary-Catherine, in particular, seemed to chatter and laugh too long and loud, as though she had grown a skin of toughness since her life on the farm. Was this what the war had done to us? Or was it her true nature?

I wasn't sure she was aware we were tailing her. She wasn't naïve, and yet she never acted as if she knew we were there. In fact, she seemed as unaffected and natural as someone with a huge secret could be.

CHAPTER 34

Wilhelm

It was dusk on the second night when it happened. We followed Mary-Catherine to the tavern and waited. Lanier brought a couple of Bureau men who went inside to make sure she didn't run out the back. Lanier told the men to follow her when she left, so that we would be positioned both in front of and behind her. We staked out in some bushes about fifty meters from the bar. A soaking October rain penetrated my clothes. Despite the cover of the bushes, I was cold, wet, and miserable. I wanted it to be over.

Two hours later the door to the pub finally opened. She was alone, which was unusual. Although this part of Chicago seemed to be safe, she had always walked with at least one other girl. I straightened and peered through the foliage. Thirty yards away a figure emerged from the shadows. A man. The same height and build as Deschler. Adrenaline shot through me. A nearby streetlight bathed his face. It *was* Deschler. I pointed.

Lanier tipped his head and mouthed, "Are you sure?"

I nodded.

Both men pulled guns from their holsters. It was the first time I'd seen them with weapons. I think both were Colt .45s, but in the dim light I couldn't be certain.

Lanier held up his hand and mouthed, "Stay."

I nodded again.

Deschler approached Mary-Catherine. Her back straightened. "What are you doing here?" Her voice was low but audible. Lanier and Cranston crept toward them, using the bushes for cover. I swallowed. The air grew charged.

Deschler leaned over to kiss her, but she stepped back to avoid the embrace.

"*Was ist?*" he asked in an equally quiet voice.

"Reinhard, the FBI and the army are close by. They know you killed a soldier at the camp."

He lurched backward. "What?" His voice carried a note of incredulity.

Schauspieler. Actor, I thought.

"They came to Mrs. Bosworth's." She planted her hands on her hips. "You lied to me!"

Lanier turned to Cranston. "Let's go. Now."

The two G-men raced down the street. "Stop!" Cranston yelled. "Don't move. Hands on your head."

Reinhard spun around. When he saw the two men advancing, he grabbed Mary-Catherine and pulled her in front of him. "*Dont nehmen einen weiteren Schritt!*" Don't take another step!

He pulled out a gun of his own and thrust it against Mary-Catherine's temple.

"You bastard!" Mary-Catherine yelled. "What are you doing? Let me go!"

"How long have you been working with—with *them?*" Deschler said.

"I'm not! They've been following me ever since you escaped. Don't you see? You walked into their trap!"

Deschler hesitated. "I cannot believe it. You have betrayed me. Why should I trust you?"

"Because you love me." Mary-Catherine swallowed. "Or so you said. I didn't betray you."

Lanier called out in a calm voice, but I noticed he still had his gun out. "Let's everyone slow down, here. Drop the gun, Deschler, so we can all live another day."

Deschler made no move to let her go. But neither did he try to harm her. As Mary-Catherine struggled, shrugging each shoulder in turn, they reversed positions. The brief glare of the streetlight reflected a panoply of emotions on Deschler's face: doubt, confusion, obstinacy.

But Mary-Catherine either couldn't or wouldn't see it. "In fact, it's the other way around. You've been using me the whole time, haven't you?" she said. "You betrayed *me.* And I fell for it. What an idiot I am."

"Mary-Catherine, stop," Deschler said. "I—I love you."

"Love? You have no idea what that word means." She shook her head as if trying to dislodge the gun against her temple. Nothing happened. At the same time, the Bureau men who'd been inside the tavern closed in behind.

Lanier spotted them. "Deschler! You're surrounded. Give it up. Let her go."

There was no answer.

"Deschler, do you hear me? It's over. Don't make it worse. Let her go."

Still no reply.

For a brief moment, I actually thought he might let her go. I dared to believe there could be a peaceful resolution.

Finally, Deschler yelled, "I cannot. I am a soldier of the Reich. We are at war."

I couldn't stay in the bushes. I hurried forward and shouted to him in German. "No, Deschler. For us the war is over. I know you understand that. There is no reason to fight. You cannot win."

He squinted into the darkness. "Is that you, Stemm?"

"Yah! Let the girl go!"

"I should have known. *You* are the traitor. It has been *you* all along, not Kohl. I killed the wrong man." He clutched the gun with one hand and pressed it more forcefully against Mary-Catherine's temple.

CHAPTER 35

Mary-Catherine

When I realized how much Reinhard had deceived me, I went rigid and clenched my fists. How dare he? I'd ruined my reputation, been run out of town, because of him. I was now working ten hours a day in a sweaty, smelly steel plant, again, because of him. A wave of hot rage swept over me. He wouldn't get away with it.

Reinhard was raving in German to Stemm. Stemm, the other German prisoner I'd talked to back at the farm. About Reinhard. I squinted, trying to make out how far away he was, but Reinhard forced the gun deeper against my temple.

I was running out of time. I needed to stall while I figured out what to do. I let myself go limp, and the G-men and Stemm started forward. I changed my tone.

"You're right, Reinhard. Stemm is a traitor. Let's get away from him. From everyone. Let's go while we still can. We can find a way out. I know it." I was babbling now, but I would say anything to get a few precious seconds.

It didn't work. I heard a click. He cocked the gun.

The men approaching us froze.

Reinhard changed direction and backtracked toward the bushes, pulling me with him.

"Back off or I kill the girl!"

A shot rang out behind us. It missed. Another bullet whizzed past my ear. Reinhard tightened his hold on me with one hand. With the other he aimed the revolver into the dark and pulled the trigger. The shot went wild.

"*Scheisse!*" he muttered.

Men now closed in from both directions. This was my chance. I slammed my elbow backward into his ribs. He stumbled. The gun flew out of his hand. I wheeled around and kneed him in the groin. He groaned and sank to the ground. His hands flew to his crotch. I bent down and grabbed the gun. The gun he'd bought with Pauline's engagement ring. I picked it up and aimed it at Reinhard.

"No!" Lanier shouted. "Don't do it, Mary-Catherine. We got him! Give me the gun!"

But before they could stop me, I fired at Reinhard three times.

CHAPTER 36

Wilhelm

Within minutes a crowd materialized in front of the tavern, pointing, calling out questions, even joking. The FBI men cuffed Mary-Catherine and locked her in the sedan. She kept her head down and never acknowledged the chorus of people asking, "What happened?" and "What did you do?"

Someone from the bar must have called the cops, because they arrived, stretched crime scene tape around Deschler's body, and moved Mary-Catherine from the FBI sedan into a patrol car. She'd killed a German traitor, but was it really self-defense? Or was it revenge? A court would determine whether she would spend the rest of her life in prison.

That night they put me up in a nice hotel but stationed a guard with me. Not Cranston or Lanier or any of the men from the bar. Just an MP. He was the chatty type, but he didn't know any German, and exhausted as I was, I couldn't muster any energy to speak in English.

I was driven to a building the next morning that turned out to be the FBI field office in downtown Chicago. When I walked in, I spotted Mrs. O'Rourke on a chair in the receptionist's area. She looked haggard and weary and wore a haunted expression.

Lanier appeared in the reception area with Cranston.

I rose from my chair. "What happens to Mary-Catherine?"

"They're holding her in a cell, but she'll probably be transferred to Cook County. She'll be charged with manslaughter—we warned her not to shoot. She might be charged with aiding and abetting the enemy as well. We're still fighting a war, you know."

Mrs. O'Rourke let out a sob and covered her face with her hands.

"But you were a hero, Stemm," Lanier went on. "We couldn't have done this without you. We will, of course, let Commander James know how helpful you were."

I didn't feel like a hero. I was imprisoned by rage, hate, and revenge—the same qualities that had triggered this war. As well as what had happened in the camp. I gazed at Mrs. O'Rourke, wishing I could comfort her. I thought about Mary-Catherine, Deschler, Kohl, Harley, even Franz. I hoped one bright, shiny day we would be free, because we were all prisoners of war.

The Day Miriam Hirsch Disappeared

THE DAY MIRIAM HIRSCH
DISAPPEARED

The day Miriam Hirsch disappeared was so hot you could almost see the sidewalk blister and sweat. It was summer 1938, and I'd been hanging around with Barney Teitelman in Lawndale, the Jewish neighborhood on Chicago's West Side. Barney's parents owned a restaurant and rooming house near Roosevelt and Kedzie. Miriam rented a room on the third floor. She was a looker, as my father would say, although if he knew his only son was spending that much time with Barney he'd have kittens.

You see, we lived in Hyde Park, a few miles and a universe away from Lawndale. We were German Jews; the Teitelmans weren't. They were from Russia or Lithuania or one of those other countries with "ia" at the end of them, and what separated us wasn't just the Austro-Hungarian Empire. We were cultured, assimilated. They were rabble. We had come over before the Civil War; they poured in at the end of the last century. We were merchants, doctors, lawyers. They worked in factories,

279

sweatshops, and, well, restaurants. In fact, when my father was being especially snooty, he'd ask which delicatessen their family owned. I, of course, disagreed with my parents. The Teitelmans talked louder and laughed more, and Mrs. T made a hell of a Shabbos brisket.

Barney and I had met by accident the previous May. We were waiting for the bus outside the College of Jewish Studies near the Loop, both of us in bow ties and yarmulkes. My parents had sent me there to "enrich" my Jewish heritage. I guess Barney's did too. We stared warily at each other for a few minutes, like dogs sniffing each other out. Then I offered him a piece of Bazooka. He took it. We were best friends.

He came to my house only once. The frosty reception my mother gave him, after he told her where he lived, was enough. There wasn't much action in Hyde Park anyway. We tried to sucker the Weinstein girls into a game of strip poker behind the rocks at the Fifty-Seventh Street beach, but they gave us the brush-off. We didn't care. They were ugly. By June, I was taking the Cottage Grove streetcar to Roosevelt and transferring west to Lawndale as often as possible.

The first time I saw Miriam, Barney and I were wolfing down brisket sandwiches in the restaurant; I could feel gravy dribbling past my chin. I heard a rustle, turned around. She was walking past our table. No, more like gliding. Dressed in a pearly gown that swept to her feet, she was perfectly proportioned, with a waist so tiny that my hands ached to encircle it, and such a generously endowed bosom that my hands ached—well, you get the idea.

Her hair was gold, her lips red, and she had the most enormous gray eyes I'd ever seen. A guy could lose his way in them.

Especially a fifteen-year-old. My mouth dropped to my chin; gravy stained my shirt. She was even carrying a parasol. I was in love.

There weren't many people in the restaurant that day, but you could feel the collective hush as she passed through. It was as if her presence had struck us dumb, and we were compelled to stare. As her skirt brushed our table, she cast a dazzling smile on Barney. He turned crimson. Then she was gone. The voltage in the air ebbed, and I heard the clink of silverware as people started to live, breathe, and eat again.

"So, who the hell was that?" I said in my best tough-guy tone.

Barney looked me over, knew I was bluffing. "Wouldn't you like to know?"

I leaned across the table and grabbed Barney's collar. "You don't tell me, Barney Teitelman, I'll tell your parents what you were trying to do to Dina Preis behind the shul last Saturday."

"You wouldn't." He didn't sound convinced.

I clutched his shirt tighter. "You got five seconds."

Barney's eyes narrowed. I guess he figured he'd better give me something. "All's I'll say is she's not for the likes of you, Jake Forman."

I dropped my hold on Barney's neck and jumped up from the table. "Mrs. T? I have something to tell you." I headed toward the kitchen.

"All right already," Barney whined. "Don't go up the wall. She's Miriam Hirsch. She's an actress with the Yiddish theater."

"When did she show up?"

"Couple days ago."

Most of the actresses at the Yiddish theater were from Eastern Europe, but Hirsch was a German name. She and I had something in common already. Then I chastised myself for doing the same thing as my parents.

"I'm gonna be an actor," I said.

Barney balled his napkin up and threw it at me.

• • •

Apparently, I wasn't the only one Miriam impressed. The next afternoon, as we were hanging out the window trying to blow cigarette smoke into the street instead of the Teitelmans' living room, Miriam came out the front door. Sun-baked heat hung in the air like a blanket, and she opened her parasol to protect her head. Halfway up, it got stuck. I was about to run down and offer my assistance when Skull cut in front of her.

Ben Skulnick, or Skull, as we called him, hung out at Davy Miller's gym and pool hall. The Miller brothers were the closest thing Lawndale had to gangsters. They'd moved over from Maxwell Street a few years earlier and built a restaurant and gambling casino next to the gym. Covering all the bases, I guess. Except the type of people who frequented the place weren't exactly high society.

Not that the Miller boys didn't have their fans. It was Davy Miller's gang who fought the uptown goyim in the twenties so that Jews could use Clarendon Beach, and it was his gang who kept all the yeshivah bochers, religious students, safe from the Irish street gangs. The scuttlebutt these days was they were going after Nazi sympathizers on the North Side. Whatever the truth, Davy Miller and his crew were proof that Jewish boys weren't sissies, a myth we were all eager to dispel.

"Look at that, Barney," I said, my eyes riveted on the scene below us.

"I see."

Tall and dark, Skull cut a dashing figure. He was probably running numbers, greasing palms, and taking cuts off the locals in the area, but with his well-trimmed whiskers, neatly pressed shirt, and Italian suit, he looked like a successful businessman, not a thug. He wore a hat, too, a snap-brimmed fedora, and moved with a sinewy grace, like a cat stalking its prey. No one knew where he came from.

"He's gonna make a play for her." I wasn't sure if I was devastated or curious.

"Do you blame him?"

We watched as he struggled with Miriam's parasol, opened it, and presented it back to her with a flourish. Before she disappeared underneath its shade, I saw the smile she gave him. And the lazy, appraising smile he gave back.

"You see that, Jake?"

I swallowed.

"Give it up, pal. You're way out of your league."

By the following week, Skull was dropping by the restaurant every afternoon. He'd order a glass of iced tea, which he tipped plenty for but never drank. Sometimes he'd grab a game of gin rummy in the back room, but mostly he checked his watch every few minutes. Around two, he'd make sure to bump into Miriam and walk her to rehearsal. And back home again later.

One evening he walked her all the way up to the third floor. That was the last we saw of them all night. Of course, Barney and I snuck up to the third-floor landing, but all we heard were strains of "Don't Be That Way" wafting down the hall from her radio. Benny Goodman. Barney dragged me back downstairs.

But I hadn't lost all hope. When Miriam's show opened, we

started to hang around the stage door of Douglas Park Auditorium to catch a glimpse of her. Skull did too. When she came out, sometimes with her stage makeup still on, he would offer her his arm and they'd saunter down the street together. Sometimes they stopped for ice cream or a sandwich at Carl's Deli. On Sundays, they headed over to the roof of the Jewish People's Institute to dance. Even at a distance, you could feel the sparks fly between them. When they smiled at each other or danced the two-step, it broke my heart. I was jealous. I was in love—with both of them. They were the epitome of glamour. They were swell. With bells on.

One night, though, was different.

"No, Skull, I won't do it." Miriam stared straight ahead as they stepped through the stage door. "Stop asking me."

There was a gleam in Skull's eye. "Oh, come on, baby, it's only for a little while."

"No." Miriam walked three steps ahead of him.

"But you're the only one who can. You speak their language."

"I don't care."

He stopped short. "How can you say that?"

"You have some chutzpah. How can you ask me to—well, to do something like that?" She whipped around to face him, her eyes flashing. Barney and I flattened ourselves against a building.

Skull backed off. His voice grew as soft as cotton. Wheedling. "You love me, don't you baby?"

She looked at him. She kept her mouth shut, but her eyes, as luminous as waves on the moonlit lake, said it all.

Skull moved in for the kill. He pushed a lock of hair off her forehead. "All I need is a little information. Then you can stop. Please. Do it for me." He paused. "For us."

Miriam pursed her lips, and I thought she was going to cry. Then she sagged against Skull, as if he had somehow managed to squeeze all the air out of her.

Skull grinned and pulled her close, planted a victory kiss on her lips. "That's my baby."

She buried her head in his shoulder. We didn't hear her reply.

• • •

Whatever Miriam agreed to that night must not have lasted long, because we never saw them together again. Skull didn't come around to Teitelmans' anymore, and he didn't show up at the auditorium. Miriam came and went by herself. Occasionally, she hailed a cab and never came home at all. It was strange, and I was confused and angry. What had Skull asked her to do? It had to be something so evil that her only recourse was to break up with him.

A week later, on an afternoon so humid that nothing felt dry, Barney and I lugged groceries past the banks on the corner. Across the street we spotted Skull getting his shoes shined. He was reading a newspaper and scowling. When he saw us he tipped his hat. Barney and I glanced at each other. Did he really mean us?

As if to answer our question, he called over to us. "Hey, Teitelman."

Barney nodded tentatively.

Skull dropped a buck in the shoeshine guy's box, overtipping as usual, and crossed the street.

"You guys been following me for a while, haven't you?"

I swallowed. Here it comes. Our first real conversation, and he's gonna tell us to butt out.

"I'm glad I run into youse. I've been meaning to call. Are youse—young gentlemen interested in a business proposition?"

My jaw dropped to my chest.

He squinted at us. "My business in other parts of the city has picked up recently and requires my—my presence there. But I still need some—whadd'ya call it—some representation here. You guys interested?" He yanked his thumb toward our bags of groceries. "Pays better than that."

I looked at Barney, then at Skull, trying to mask my excitement with a shrug. It didn't work. A soft yelp escaped my mouth.

"Good. Come around to Miller's at three." Skull turned on his heel, dropping the paper in the trash on the corner. I glanced at the headline—something about hooligans throwing rocks at a group of German-American Bund members on the North Side.

The long and the short of it was that Skull wanted us to do errands for him in the neighborhood. Nothing major, just running messages to Zookie the Bookie and picking up envelopes from some of the shops. At first he came with us to show us the ropes. Then we were on our own.

It was a fair trade-off. We didn't have Miriam, but we did have Skull. In some ways, it was better. We were important. Even the guys in the pool hall nodded to us after a while. And we were making great money. Almost ten bucks a day. Barney and I made up new names for each other. I was Jake the Snake; he was Barney Bow Tie.

On the days Skull was with us, I watched him operate. He was smooth. He'd flash one of his lazy smiles, and even the people he was bilking smiled back. Especially the ladies. The only time he lost his cool was the afternoon we passed Miriam. She was crossing the street to catch a cab. Their eyes met, and I thought I saw a look of infinite sadness, passion, and what-might-have-been pass between them. How could it be over, with looks like that?

• • •

I should have known it wouldn't last. One morning in late July my mother and father woke me up. Poised for attack, they stood at the foot of my bed.

"Jacob, you have some explaining to do." My mother's eyes were cold steel.

I tried to play dumb. "What's that, Ma?" I yawned. Slowly.

"Just exactly what have you been doing in Lawndale?"

"What do you mean?"

"Jacob, don't try to weasel your way out of this one." My father glared. "Henry Solomon saw you outside Davy Miller's the other day. How long have you been consorting with gangsters?"

"Gangsters? What gangsters?"

My father cut me off. "You want to play it that way? Fine. You're forbidden to go there anymore."

"But Barney's my best friend."

"He's a bad influence. They all are." My father wheeled around as if there was nothing more to say.

"But I've got a job. I'm making good money."

"Good money?" My father whipped back around. His face was purple. "That kind of money you don't need. You want a job, you work in Kahn's bakery. It was good enough for me—it'll do for you."

I wanted to ask him why he figured Henry Solomon, one of our most respectable Hyde Park neighbors, was over in Lawndale, but somehow I didn't think the time was right.

• • •

If the boredom didn't get me, the pretense did. Life in Hyde Park was intolerable. And hot. Not even a wisp of a breeze fluttered through the curtains of our wide-open windows. About a week later, it got so bad even my parents took off for the Michigan shore. I pled a toothache. As soon as they left, not without suspicious glances at the ice pack clamped to my cheek, I hopped the streetcar over to Lawndale. Mrs. Teitelman was washing the floor of the restaurant.

"Where have you been, Jake? Barney's at a concert in Douglas Park. You just missed him."

"I'll wait." I looked around. The place was empty. I snuck a glance at the door leading to the stairs.

"How are things?"

Mrs. Teitelman followed my gaze. She shrugged, a grim set to her mouth.

"Did Skull come back?"

Another shrug.

I was just breaking out a bottle of seltzer when the door to the stairs opened, and a man crossed the restaurant. He had blond whiskers, a round red face, and an odd twitch in one eye. He didn't look Jewish. He hurried across the room, staring straight ahead, as if he knew he didn't belong and wanted to get out fast.

A few minutes later, Miriam skipped down the steps, her smile as bright as a box of new Shabbos candles. I froze. Who was this impostor? Where was Skull? I felt betrayed. She waved at me before gliding out the door.

Barney got back from the park around four.

"What's been going on around here?" I asked.

"I don't know." He hung his head as if he were responsible for the turn of events.

"Didn't they get back together?"

"Nope. He hasn't been here at all. In fact—"

"What?" I was starting to feel panicky.

"I dunno, Jake. Sometimes she doesn't come home at night. And then one time, her eyes were all red rimmed like she'd been crying, and her dress was ripped. She didn't even have her key. My father had to let her in."

"Jesus, Barney."

He nodded. "And when she's here, she's 'entertaining' in her room. But it isn't Skull."

"The guy I saw earlier?"

"Yeah. I think he's goyim. Mother's ready to kick her out."

I turned to Mrs. T in desperation. "You can't do that. Where will she go?"

Mrs. T just looked at me. "Jacob, there are some things you're still too young to understand."

That afternoon we ran down to the pool hall and caught up with Skull at Miller's. We were sweating like pigs, but he was cool and dapper.

"Where ya bin, Snake?" He grinned.

"I was grounded, Skull. My parents." I rolled my eyes.

He looked at me speculatively. "Your parents must be real Nervous Nellies."

"They're German," I admitted.

"So are Miriam's," Skull said. "Crabbers. Stiff as sandpaper."

I took that as an opening and screwed up my courage. "How is Miriam these days?"

He ignored my question. "You know, it's a damn shame about

you Yeccas." That was slang for German Jews. "One of the best guys I ever heard of was Arnold Rothstein. Practically started the Mafia. His family was German, but he was tops. You know what he did?"

I shook my head.

"Hustled the most famous pool shark in the country. Beat his *tuchus* off. And he hardly even played pool."

"How'd he do that?"

"Kept the guy up until he won. Forty hours with no sleep." Skull winked at me. "Rothstein had style, too. He ran a casino, moved a lot of booze, financed all sorts of capers. But he always wore a tux and he danced with the ladies every night." Skull's chin dipped. "He was—whadda'ya call it—a smooth operator."

I wanted to ask him more about Miriam, but I didn't have the guts.

• • •

Mrs. T never had the chance to evict Miriam. She never came back. Three days later they found her body in an alley off Lincoln Avenue. The German part of town. She'd been raped, beaten, strangled. The cops identified her by her purse.

A tough-looking Irish detective, Patrick O'Meara, came around to question us. Mrs. T told him everything she knew. About the theater. Skull. The man with the blond whiskers.

O'Meara hustled over to Davy Miller's to question Skull. We trailed behind. It was the first time we'd seen him ourselves in a couple of days. He looked bad. His shirt was wrinkled, he hadn't shaved, and his bloodshot eyes kept darting around the room. His mood seemed to shift from arrogance to desolation, and his answers were clipped and curt.

I began to think the worst. Miriam and Skull had broken up. Miriam had started up with other men. Skull must have been crazy with jealousy and he snapped. It looked that way to me. And to O'Meara. He wasn't nice to Skull. Told him not to go anywhere for a while.

Of course, the next morning Skull was gone, and no one knew where. Or they weren't telling. That was the only proof I needed. He'd killed Miriam. Maybe my parents were right after all. Lawndale people were different.

Barney and I were puzzling it over at the restaurant when O'Meara showed up. Mrs. T was upstairs getting dressed, so he nabbed Joey, the headwaiter.

"Ever seen this guy?" He showed him a picture.

Joey shook his head.

"You sure?" You could tell O'Meara didn't believe him. "Seen Skulnick recently?"

Joey kept wiping glasses with his towel. "Nope."

O'Meara turned around, saw us sitting at a table. We froze. His eyes narrowed; then he came over. I tried to look nonchalant.

"Your turn, boys. You ever seen this guy?"

He threw the picture down on our table.

I could hear Barney's sharp intake of breath. It was the man with the blond whiskers. I tried to be blasé.

But O'Meara was patient. Eventually, my eyes drifted back to the picture. O'Meara was waiting.

"So what's it gonna be, boys?"

"Who is he?" I croaked.

"You seen him?"

I met O'Meara's eyes and nodded.

"Name's Peter Schultz. They call him Twitch. Some kind of

problem around his eye." O'Meara stared at me. I looked at the floor. I knew the name. Peter Schultz was one of the leaders of the German-American Bund in Chicago. They were Nazis.

"He was murdered last night," O'Meara said. "We found him in the same alley they found the girl."

Barney made a mewling sound in his throat. I felt old.

"He was stabbed about fifteen times, then strangled. They got him pretty good."

I didn't move.

O'Meara kept the pressure on. "You know, it's interesting. With him gone, their whole organization is up for grabs, you know?"

I didn't say anything, but the pieces were finally coming together. I knew who killed Miriam, and I knew who killed Schultz. I wondered if O'Meara knew too.

O'Meara went on. "Someone—someone close to him—knew the Kraut's habits so well they even knew what time he took a dump. They got him on his way to a Bund meeting. You have any idea who that might be?"

I kept my mouth shut.

He shook his head. "Well, whoever it was, now there's one less Nazi in the world." O'Meara stood up, put his hat on, threw us a world-weary glance. "They say all's fair in love and war. What do you think?"

What I thought was that I may have been wrong about Skull all along; that this was more about war than love. There may have been a reason why Miriam was dating Schultz; why Skull was pressuring Miriam to get information she didn't want to. While Skull used Miriam, he was also her avenger.

"I'll be seeing you boys around," O'Meara said, then stepped through the door and left.

•••

Skull never came back to Lawndale. At least we never heard from him again. I didn't hang around much either. School started, and I got busy with homework and sports. I met a girl at Hyde Park High, Barbara Steinberg. She was pretty nice. Barney called a couple of times, but neither of us pushed it. Other things were fast taking precedence. Hitler annexed Austria, and the news coming out of Europe was grim. No one seemed to remember the day Miriam Hirsch disappeared.

Acknowledgements

Many Americans, especially those born after World War II, do not know that from 1943 through 1945, more than half a million German (and Italian) prisoners of war were housed here in the US. My state of Illinois alone ran five or more camps, and only four states did not host any. The US Army, which had authority over the POWs, followed the Geneva Conventions to the letter, with the result that many Germans were treated better than they were in their own military and did not want to return home after war's end. *POW* is based on a true incident, although I have taken considerable liberties with the facts. I am indebted to James Maierhoff, from the University of Illinois, Chicago, who studies the archeology of POW camps in Illinois.

Thanks also must go to Jan Gordon, editor extraordinaire, who read both novellas and provided much-needed developmental suggestions, as well as my writing group, the Red Herrings, who, collectively, are sharper than I at finding what doesn't work. Twenty years and still going strong.

Thanks for reading *War, Spies, & Bobby Sox*. If you enjoyed it, please consider leaving a review at your favorite retailer and/or Goodreads.

And to find out more about Libby, contact her at the following places:

libbyhellmann.com

facebook.com/authorlibbyfischerhellmann

twitter.com/libbyhellman

11/17

Made in the USA
Columbia, SC
03 November 2017